MOON SEVERED

Mirror Lake Wolves - Book Three

JENNIFER SNYDER

MOON SEVERED
MIRROR LAKE WOLVES – BOOK THREE

Editing by H. Danielle Crabtree

ISBN-13: 978-1981306411
ISBN-10: 1981306412

1

Two days passed before Violet woke. Three before Drew's body was found. Alec had been the one to tell me he'd been found dead, but even if he hadn't I would've heard about it anyway. Rumors flew around town like wildfire, spreading with each person's heated breath.

Mirror Lake hadn't seen something so *tragic* in years. At least not among the humans. The supernaturals? We were used to it.

Even so, it still shook me up. Maybe it was because of everything I knew firsthand surrounding Drew's death, or maybe it was because Shane had found him. As much as I didn't care for Shane, finding someone you loved dead wasn't something I would wish on anyone. Not even someone who was more foe than friend. I could only imagine how the memory would tarnish all others of that person. How it would haunt him for the rest of his life.

No one deserved that. Not even Shane.

I sent Becca a message telling her I was sorry about

Shane's brother. It seemed like the thing to do. Silence felt as though it would imply guilt, and I didn't need any more than what I already harbored.

The news of Violet waking had been darkened by Drew's discovery, causing my emotions to give me whiplash. Tension had melted away as gratitude slipped in only to be eaten to bits of nothing when I got the text from Alec telling me Shane had found his brother dead.

The image of Eli snapping Drew's neck had flashed through my mind on repeat since. The memory more vulgar and violent than the actual act.

Apparently, guilt could do that to a memory.

They found him. If we just lie low this will all die down soon. Remember he'd already hurt Violet. He planned to hurt you next. And who knows how many more members of our pack he would have hurt if I hadn't stopped him.

The text was from Eli. It came through as I stared at Alec's announcement of Drew's death. My face scrunched up as a lump built in the back of my throat. The image of Eli snapping Drew's neck shifted to Violet in the cage. Her mangled ankle. Her bruised and marred skin. I remembered how I'd thought she was dead, but how it turned out Drew had drugged her. Anger lapped at my insides.

Then I remembered Drew was dead, which meant the threat he placed on our pack had died along with him.

As sick as it might seem, a small sense of comfort slithered through my veins at the thought.

Until Shane entered my mind.

My heart kicked into overdrive as I wondered what went

through his head. Had he thought of the pack? Did he think one of us had killed Drew in retaliation for what he'd done? Did he think it was me?

Don't beat yourself up over this, Mina. We only did what had to be done. For the pack.

I reread Eli's last message, knowing he was right. Drew had to die for the safety of the pack. He wasn't one who could have been silenced by the fear of what we were or what we could do to him, because he already knew and he wasn't afraid. What he'd been doing proved it.

My mind drifted back to Shane.

Would we be able to scare him into submission so he left us alone? Or would drastic measures have to be taken with him too? I forced the thought away. I couldn't think about it. Yeah, I didn't like the guy, but that didn't mean I wanted him to die. He was young. Younger than his brother who should've known better.

My mind took me back to the night Eli and I hid in the woods, the night we overheard the conversation between Shane and Drew about their plan. Shane hadn't seemed as confident as his brother about what they were doing. He'd seemed scared. Or maybe somewhere deep inside him there were actual morals and what Drew was doing crossed them. If I was wrong, then fear would be our best motivator when it came to him. Especially now that we'd killed his brother.

My thumbs tapped across the screen of my cell as I replied to Eli's text.

I'm not beating myself up. I was there. I know it had to be done. - Mina

There was truth in my words but also lies. Even as I read

the text again, I couldn't distinguish which was which. There was a good chance Eli wouldn't be able to either.

What time do you want to visit Violet? - Mina

I asked for a swift change of subject. I needed to think of something else.

It had been a solid day since Violet woke. Gran had insisted we give her time before we bombarded her with questions about what happened.

Now. Let's go.

The breath I'd been holding expelled from my lungs. Thank goodness he wanted to go now. I didn't think I could wait another second. I wanted to know everything Violet knew. I needed to. Information was the only thing that was going to keep me sane. It was the only thing that could act as kryptonite to the guilt I felt surrounding Drew's death.

I'll meet you there. – Mina

I shoved my cell into the back pocket of my shorts and swiped a hair tie from my dresser. The desire to look into the mirror was too much of a draw to resist. As I piled my mop of long hair on top of my head, I cast a quick glance at myself. My eyes were darker than usual. Worry lines creased the area between my brows and forced my lips into a thin line.

I was the walking definition of guilt.

Inhaling a deep breath, I forced my face to relax. The tension in my shoulders eased as the worry lines between my brows faded. My eyes didn't brighten, but hopefully no one would notice.

Another text came through on my cell. The soft chime of it startled me enough to allow the mask I was building to fall away.

No need. I'm at your front door.

Relief trickled through me. Maybe it was wrong, but Eli's presence felt like a sedative to my frazzled nerves. Thankfully because I had been about to raid Gran's herbal pantry for something to help chill me out. Knowing me, I'd botch it and place myself in a coma. Herbs weren't my forte.

Guess Eli was good for something.

That was an unnecessary jab; Eli was good for many things. But I was just now realizing this.

I shoved my cell in my pocket. A whimper at my feet caught my attention. It was Gracie's little fur ball. His large brown eyes got me, and I bent to scoop him up. Even though I'd never admit it to anyone, I was grateful for the little guy. It was nice to have someone around who didn't talk, didn't drink alcohol, and didn't expect anything from me other than to show a little affection from time to time.

"Don't worry, little buddy. She'll be home soon," I told Winston as I scratched behind his ear while hugging him to my chest. "I promise."

Gracie had spent a lot of time at Callie's lately. I understood. Callie was her best friend, and her family was going through a lot. Gran had agreed Gracie could stay with Callie for moral support through today. After today she'd have to come home so Violet's family could spend uninterrupted time with her. Gracie understood. She was a good kid. A smart one. At thirteen, she was wise beyond her years. In fact, it hadn't taken her long to figure out something horrible had happened to Violet. She knew the story of her getting lost in the woods during a run alone wasn't the truth. There was no doubt in my mind Eli and me coming over today to talk to Violet would solidify that. Gracie would have questions, ones

I wouldn't be able to answer. Unless Eli said I could fill her in. Pack law had been in place regarding the situation since the beginning.

I placed Winston in his crate. His high-pitched, yippy bark echoed through our room. I hated locking him up. It reminded me too much of how we'd found Violet. Leaving Winston like this seemed cruel, but it was for the best. There was no telling what he would chew up or piss all over while we were all gone.

"It's okay. Gracie will be home soon. Chill out, little buddy. You won't be in there forever," I said as I pulled the striped beach towel over his crate so he couldn't see anymore.

It didn't help. In fact, it only pissed him off more. His bark became louder, and he scratched at the floor of his cage aggressively. My heart broke for him. Sometime over the last week, I'd grown to care for him. He was cute. There was no denying it. He also wasn't as much work as I'd thought he would be. He had a good temperament, and he listened decently well for his age.

I backed away from the cage and headed down the hall toward the front door. Eli was waiting. Even if he hadn't told me he was at my front door, I would have known.

I could feel him.

I opened the front door and stepped down the stairs. Eli was leaning against my car, waiting on me. He was dressed in a pair of gray cargo shorts and a thin ribbed white tank top. It seemed to be his signature look lately. I didn't mind. It showcased his muscles.

"Hey," he said. "Sounds like someone misses you." The corners of his lips quirked into a ghost of a smile. It was a jab at me. He knew I didn't like dogs, but what he didn't know was that this one had wormed his way into my heart somehow.

"He doesn't miss me," I muttered. Gravel crunched beneath my sandals as I walked past him toward the Marshalls' trailer. "He's pissed I locked him in his crate."

Eli caught up to me and matched his pace to mine. "Keep telling yourself that and maybe you'll believe it."

I rolled my eyes.

When we were halfway to Violet's, I risked a glance at Eli. His brows were pinched together in deep thought as he chewed the inside of his cheek. Was he nervous to talk to Violet? Was he worried she wouldn't have any new information?

His eyes shifted to mine, catching me staring. I blinked and looked away.

"Do you think she'll remember anything?" I asked. I had to say something. The silence between us was deafening.

"I hope so."

"What are you hoping she'll remember?" I asked as we neared the cinderblock steps that led to her front door. The steps were the only thing that made the Marshalls' place look temporary. Everything else about it seemed permanent. It was well cared for. In fact, it was one of the nicer trailers in the park. Navy blue shutters that matched the color of the front door hung beside all the windows. Mrs. Marshall had a beautiful raised flower bed that ran along the length of the front. Each spring she planted flowers in various colors. I asked her once why she didn't buy perennials knowing it would save her a lot of work, time, and money. She told me planting them again every year satisfied her need for change.

She could change the color. She could change the height of the plants. She liked that.

"I hope she remembers something about where Drew took Glenn. I hope she can give us more information on who's running this thing." His professional tone irked me. He was no longer just Eli. In the span of a few steps, he'd somehow switched to being the alpha's son on a mission.

I started up the cinderblock stairs that led to the Marshalls' front door and knocked.

Gracie stepped to the screen door and motioned for me to step inside. She looked upset. "Violet is in the back."

What was she upset about? Shouldn't she be happy?

Callie caught my eye when I stepped inside. She was on the couch with her legs tucked beneath her. She looked worse than Gracie. What was wrong? Why weren't they happy Violet was finally awake? Had something happened?

I started for the hall. The air was thick and charged with energy. Something was wrong. I could feel it as I inched toward the bedroom at the end.

"Something isn't right," Eli said, confirming my fear. "The energy here is too frantic."

"I know." I nodded in agreement.

The sharp scent of herbs lingered in the air near the door. Gran was inside, working her magic. I knew she was here checking on Violet, but I had no idea she'd be doing any sort of healing for her. Honestly, I thought we were beyond that. Apparently, we weren't.

"The lavender should help, but I think the tea will help even more." Gran's whispered words had my feet faltering. "She should be okay. We have to remember, she suffered a traumatic experience. In situations like this, it's not uncommon for abilities to behave this way."

To behave what way? Was Violet okay?

My mind raced with questions as I picked apart Gran's tone.

She was worried. About Violet.

Why?

2

I could count on one hand how many times in my life I'd heard Gran sound as worried as she did now. Most of them were in relation to my dad and his excessive drinking, his disability, and his broken heart over my mom leaving us. Never had I heard her sound so heart stricken about someone else in the pack.

The ajar door to Violet's bedroom swung open, and Gran stepped out. Her eyes locked with mine, and I saw exactly how worried she was for Violet before she could put up her walls.

"Mina," she breathed as her hand flew to her chest. "You startled me. I didn't know the two of you were here yet."

"We just got here. We wanted to visit Violet." The words slipped from my mouth before any question surging through my mind could.

Gran closed the door behind her. "I'm not sure Violet is up for visitors today."

"We have questions about what happened, about the

abduction," Eli insisted from where he stood behind me. His chest brushed against me as he moved closer.

"I don't think that's a good idea. She needs more time to recover." Gran folded her arms over her chest and flashed us a stern look, one I knew well. It meant there would be no negotiating with her. She'd made up her mind. No one was visiting Violet today to ask her any questions about what happened.

"This is pack business, and I'm sorry, but you don't have a say in the matter." Eli's voice was filled with authority. It had goose bumps prickling across my skin.

Gran unfolded her arms. Her chin lifted, and for a moment, I thought she was going to tell Eli where he could go for using that tone with her, but she didn't. Instead she stepped aside and swung the door open for us without a word.

"Thank you," Eli said as he squeezed past both of us and into Violet's room.

"Gran, I—"

"Don't." She held up a hand to stop my flow of words. "I don't need any apology from you. I don't need excuses or reasoning. I've told you Violet isn't up to taking visitors today. She's not well, but you've insisted on carrying out whatever pack business you're on. I'll be at home, making a few tinctures that hopefully will help heal Violet's mind, body, and soul sometime soon."

Gran started down the hall without another word. I remained mute and frozen. Never had I seen her so upset with me before. When she was out of sight, I stepped into Violet's room. No matter how much Gran wanted me not to bother Violet today, we needed to. I had questions only she could answer.

Violet sat on her bed. Her foot was propped up on a stack of pillows, and there was a goopy paste the color of baby poop smeared over her ankle. The aroma of herbs hung heavily in the air, but I couldn't distinguish one from the other to determine what Gran had used. A steaming mug of tea was clasp between Violet's hands as she gingerly sipped its contents. Silver jewelry adorned each of her fingers as well as her wrists. She reminded me of a boho princess. My gaze traveled up her arms. The bruises there had barely faded. Why? Was her werewolf healing not working? From the looks of her, it didn't seem as though it was. She should have been healed by now, but she wasn't.

This couldn't be good.

"Hello, Mina. It's nice of you to stop by," Mrs. Marshall said as I stepped farther into the room. "I don't think I'll ever be able to thank you enough for helping to bring my little girl home."

"You're welcome," I said with a small smile as I moved my attention from Violet to Mrs. Marshall. The woman didn't look as though she'd slept in days. One would think she'd be sleeping better now that her daughter was home safe and sound; however, that didn't seem to be the case. "I'm glad I was able to help."

"I know this is a difficult time, and were this situation any less grave or severe I would give it more time before asking Violet questions, but unfortunately we don't have that luxury," Eli said in a soft, soothing voice.

Even though there was a part of me that didn't appreciate the way he cut straight to it, I knew it was probably for the best. We needed information, and we needed it fast if we were going find Glenn or figure out who was behind all of this. I hoped Violet had heard a name during her time with Drew. Preferably of the one running the show.

"I know." Mrs. Marshall nodded.

Eli shifted his attention to Violet. "Is there anything you can tell me about your time spent with the guy who abducted you?"

Violet sipped her tea. Her glassy eyes stared at the thin blanket spread across the upper portion of her legs. What had Gran given her? A sedative for anxiety? I knew she'd spoken since waking. Gracie said when she finally woke she'd babbled about all sorts of stuff. None of it had made sense, but at least we knew she could speak still.

"Anything at all. It doesn't matter if it's small or seemingly insignificant. Any information you can give would be better than nothing," Eli pressed.

Violet remained unresponsive.

My skin tingled as the silence dragged on. Something was wrong with her. Shock? Or something worse? Had whatever Drew did to her broken her in some way? Or was this because of the drug he'd given her?

I stepped to where Eli stood and placed a hand on his shoulder, wanting him to step back and let me have a shot. He gave me some space, and I positioned myself on the edge of her bed. My hand reached out to cover hers. She was cold to the touch.

"I know what you went through was traumatic, but I want you to know the guy who did this can't hurt you anymore. Eli and I made sure of that the night we rescued you." My voice was soft as I leaned forward. I knew she needed to hear my words. Hell, her mom probably needed to hear them too. I hoped my words assuaged her fear. "You're safe. He can't hurt you anymore." I repeated it because it felt necessary.

Violet blinked and her fingers twitched, clinking a couple rings against her mug. I assumed she was going to take another sip of tea, but instead, she shifted to look me in the eye. Her wide eyes glistened with unshed tears as her lips quivered.

My heart broke for her.

"It's okay," I whispered as I held her stare. "You're home now. With your family. With your pack."

"Mina is right. This is a safe place," Eli insisted as he crouched down beside me. His hand gripped the edge of her bed, and my body became acutely aware of the mere inches separating my knee from the tips of his fingers. "Is there anything you can remember from that night we might be able to use to figure out who the person in charge was?"

Whispered words flowed past Violet's lips. I could barely make out what she'd said, but when I focused hard enough, her words made my heart stop.

"He wanted you," Violet repeated. "Not me. It wasn't supposed to be me. It was supposed to be you."

I knew this, but it still didn't lessen the blow that came with hearing her words out loud. Of course Drew had wanted me. That was why Shane had been so smug that night. He thought it would be the last time he ever had to lay eyes on me.

"I saw him watching you. Pure evil in his eyes. He hates what we are. He hates us. I didn't have to hear him say the words to know. I could feel it in the air around him. Hatred is a strong emotion when it's deeply rooted inside a person," Violet muttered as she placed the teacup to her lips. She took a small sip as the rest of us waited for her to continue. Her gaze drifted to me before she spoke again. "I should've listened to you. When I saw you in the woods I should have headed home, but I didn't."

"You were there?" Mrs. Marshall demanded. She'd remained silent until now, but I didn't blame her for speaking up. "You saw her in the woods, running alone and shifted? You told her to go home? Why didn't you say anything to me or my husband? To Callie?"

I didn't know what to say. Awful didn't do justice to describe how I felt.

"She was told not to," Eli said. His words were firm but not harsh. I shifted to glance at him, wanting to thank him for sticking up for me, but his gaze was locked on Violet. "Do you know why you were taken instead of Mina? Did he say?"

"I was weaker," she said matter-of-factly. I was surprised by how easily the words rolled off her tongue. "Mina is strong. She's a fighter. The guy who abducted me knew this. He brought two tranquilizers for her. He only had to use one on me..."

I wanted to tell her she wasn't weak, that the other tranquilizer had been used on Tate, but Eli flashed me a look that told me I should be quiet.

"Did he tell you what he intended to do with you?" Eli asked. I knew he was only asking to keep her talking, but I hated the way he'd worded the question.

When Violet's eyes lifted to find mine again, anger flared within their color. The air seemed to grow thick as it became charged with her rage.

"He was going to sell me," Violet insisted, her eyes never wavering from mine. "But he was going to do much worse to you. He watched you pretend to be normal, human, with his brother's friend, and he didn't like it."

Eli tensed beside me as a shiver slipped up my spine. I hadn't realized Drew held such hatred for me. Was that how Shane felt too?

Deep down, I knew the answer.

I forced my thoughts away. Drew was dead, and Shane didn't matter right now. Violet did. We needed to figure out who was behind all of this. They needed to be stopped.

"Do you know who he planned to sell you to?" Eli asked, keeping us on track with gaining new information. "Did you hear anything pertaining to the person in charge?"

Violet took a sip from her tea. Her eyes glassed over again, and for a second time I wondered what herbs Gran had used in her drink. Whatever it was it must have been something good, because each time she took a sip, she looked as though she were high on something.

"No. I don't know who he wanted to sell me to," Violet insisted. "But I think there was more than one person involved."

"What do you mean? Was he talking to more than one person on the phone? Or did more than one person stop by his house while you were being held there?" Eli asked.

Violet shook her head. "No. It was something he said. It sounded like he was double-crossing someone. He mentioned being afraid to have me at his place for long because they might find out. I can't remember much. The tranquilizer he gave me was strong, but I know he said something along those lines when he left a message with someone on the phone."

"There had to be a middleman to the whole operation then," I said. "That must be who Drew was talking to."

My mind raced with how big this situation might be. Eli and I might have bitten off more than we could chew.

"I never heard him say any names or places, though." Violet shifted around on her bed. She winced from the movement, and I was reminded again that she wasn't healing properly.

After I left here I planned to head home and talk with Gran. I wanted to know more about how Violet was doing health wise.

"I'm sorry but I don't know anything more," Violet insisted.

"Okay. If you think of anything, please let us know," Eli said as he stood.

It didn't go unnoticed the way he'd said *us* instead of *me.* We were in this together. I was glad he'd realized not including me was a deal breaker. I needed to see this all play out. I needed to know who was running it. I needed to help find Glenn.

"I will," Violet insisted before she took another sip of tea.

"I'll see you out," Mrs. Marshall said as she motioned us toward the door. We stepped into the hallway, and she closed the door behind us. When she spun around to face us, a look of worry pinched her features. "Is the person who did this to my little girl really no longer a threat?" she whispered.

I should've known the question would come. It was one any mother would think to ask, but still I hadn't been prepared for it. My tongue was like sandpaper against the roof of my mouth as I thought of how to answer.

"Yes, he truly is no longer a threat," Eli answered for me.

Mrs. Marshall's eyes zeroed in on him. A wild look flared within them that made unease prickle along my skin. "Did that dead Hopkins boy they found have anything to do with this?"

I couldn't breathe. I should've known people in the pack would piece it together on their own. Drew's death had been ruled an accident, which was exactly what we'd staged, but that didn't mean everyone would believe it. Especially not when one of our own had been rescued days before someone in town turned up dead.

"I'm not at liberty to say," Eli insisted. "Pack business. I'm sorry."

Mrs. Marshall soaked in Eli's reply. Her face shifted through a handful of emotions before settling on one—displeasure. Eli's answer hadn't been satisfying enough for her. She wanted a person to blame. A face and name. I understood, but I also felt it was better she didn't know. Knowing the one responsible had been taken care of, that he was no longer a threat, should be enough to satisfy her.

For anyone normal it would have been, but Mrs. Marshall was different. She was a werewolf, and just like the others in the trailer park, when one of our own had been hurt, we wanted to hunt down the person responsible and take justice into our own hands.

Eli started down the hall and I followed.

Gracie was on the couch beside Callie when we stepped into the living room of their single wide trailer. Her eyes flicked to me. I could see questions for me building in them. She wanted to know if I knew what was wrong with Violet. She wanted to know if she was right in thinking something was wrong. I chewed my bottom lip and held her stare.

Maybe it would be enough to get my answer across to her without using words.

Something was definitely wrong with Violet. She wasn't healing like she should, and I wasn't one hundred percent sure the glassy look in her eyes was all Gran's tea either.

Violet looked lost. Broken.

I needed to speak with Gran. I needed to know what her thoughts were on this. Mainly because a part of me still felt responsible for what happened to Violet. Maybe a part of me always would.

3

"I'm going to check in with my dad," Eli said as we left Violet's. "Update him."

Gracie had opted to stay behind so she could spend more time with Callie before coming home for the night. She'd asked if I would check on Winston again for her.

I'd agreed to, of course. The little guy was growing on me.

"Update him on what?" I asked.

"Everything. He's been away handling another pack-related issue." He paused and scratched his head. "I haven't been able to fill him in on anything."

Our alpha was always dealing with something besides this situation. I knew he'd placed Eli on this, but I still couldn't help but wonder what he could be handling that was more important. "Does he know we rescued Violet?"

"He knows she was found and that she's alive. He doesn't know any details, though."

"That's going to be a long conversation."

A smirk twisted at the corners of Eli's mouth. "Yeah, you can say that again."

I crammed my hands into the back pockets of my shorts as we paused in the space that separated my Gran's trailer from his parents. A long breath expelled from my lungs. "Well, good luck."

"Thanks," Eli said. "I'm hoping he has some advice for us."

"That would be nice."

We were back to square one. Violet hadn't known anything that would help move this along. Which meant the only thing we had left in our tool belt was Peter, Shane's oldest brother. We hadn't searched his place yet.

"I'll catch up with you later," Eli insisted. His voice sounded odd.

Was he worried about what his dad might say once he learned how far Eli had gone to rescue Violet?

"You better. I want to know how it goes with your dad." I hoped he wasn't too hard on him. Killing someone—human or other—wasn't something to ever be taken lightly, regardless of the situation. "I guess I'll head inside and talk with Gran about Violet. Find out what's going on with her. Didn't you think there was something wrong with her? I mean she should be healed by now, shouldn't she?" My brows furrowed as I thought about the bruises and scratches on her still.

"Her ankle, no. That'll probably take time. Heck, you know as well as I do that when someone suffers a severe injury while in their human form nine times out of ten their wolf healing doesn't kick in to heal them."

"I know," I said, knowing he was referencing my father's

accident. "I'm talking about the cuts and bruises. Those should have been healed days ago."

Eli scratched his brow. "Yeah, I figured they would have been gone before we found her."

"I don't understand it, but..." I nodded toward Gran's trailer. "I'm about to find out what's going on."

"If you learn anything, let me know, will you?"

"Sure," I said as I stepped toward the stairs that led to my front door. "Keep me posted on the conversation with your dad, okay?"

"Maybe you should come over later tonight so you can fill me in and vice versa," he said as his gaze locked with mine. "You can take a couple more sips from a volcano's ass with me." He winked as he started walking backward toward his parents' trailer.

I didn't say a word. Instead, I pretended to be thinking long and hard about his offer as I watched him walk away. A smile stretched across my face before he disappeared around the front of his parents' trailer.

Nervous butterflies fluttered through my stomach. Not for the conversation I was about to have with Gran, but for Eli's conversation with his dad. I couldn't imagine how he must be feeling. He was about to tell his dad he'd killed someone. Maybe it wouldn't be so bad. I was sure Eli's dad had taken care of a few people in his position as alpha for the safety of the pack.

Even so, it still didn't seem to justify a life being taken.

I stepped inside Gran's place. A familiar scent made its way to my nose. I closed the door behind me. Gran was in the kitchen, concocting something made of herbs at the stove. I knew whatever she was making was for Violet.

"Are you done interrogating Violet for today?" she asked without glancing at me. Her tone was sharp. Even if I hadn't noticed it, I would have known she was upset with me. I could sense her anger. It rolled off her in waves and lingered in the air alongside the heavy scent of herbs.

"We weren't interrogating her," I said as nicely as I could manage.

Gran shifted to face me, one of her brows arched high. "If you honestly don't think what you were doing was interrogating the poor girl, then what do you call it?"

"Gathering information," I said with a shrug.

"Exactly, interrogation." Gran pursed her lips together as a look of heated irritation flashed through her eyes. Her anger didn't last long. It dissipated quicker than I would have thought possible. "I know you're working with Eli on this—whatever it is—and while I'm grateful you're finally spending time with him, I wish you would've let Violet rest another day or two before you decided to bombard her with questions. The girl's not well, Mina."

My throat grew thick. "What's wrong with her? I know something's off, but I can't put my finger on what." I crossed into the kitchen and propped my hip against the counter. "She should be healed, but she's not."

"Well, her ankle was pretty bad. It will take time," Gran said as she continued stirring whatever she was heating on the stove. From where I stood, I could see a thick, brown substance in the pot. One that reminded me of dark molasses. "But it's her bruises and cuts still being present that concerns me."

"Do you think whatever drug she was given did something to her healing abilities?"

Gran shook her head. "No. I don't think that has anything to do with it. I think it has more to do with how long she was left without silver touching her skin."

Silver. I'd forgotten she hadn't been wearing any when we found her. The bars of the cage she'd been locked in had been made of iron.

Had Drew known what silver did to us and how much we needed it? Could he have been that smart?

"I think Violet is having issues healing because being without silver for so long severed her from her wolf," Gran said.

My heart hammered against my ribs. I'd never known anyone to become severed from her wolf before, but always knew it was possible.

Poor Violet. An image of her on her bed looking utterly broken flashed through my mind. Her potentially being severed from her wolf made the sight of all her silver jewelry make sense.

"How do we fix it? Fix her?" Panic settled inside me. Was there a way to fix this?

"Honestly, Mina, I'm not sure. I've never dealt with this before. All I can think to do is place as much silver around her as possible, keep giving her tea to calm her nerves, and pray to the moon goddess whatever has happened to her reverses itself in time." Gran turned off the stove and poured the thick syrup she'd been stirring into a glass brown bottle. "You know as well as I do silver tethers the wolf to our human form. It keeps us connected. A way to keep our wolf close if we should need it. Take that away, and the connection, the bond, the tether fades until it disappears altogether."

"Are you saying Violet's wolf is gone forever?"

Gran shook her head as she twisted a dropper lid onto the brown bottle. "I'm not saying anything. I don't know much about this situation. It's all new territory. Her wolf could be gone for good or just lost." She reached for a paper towel and moved to wipe up the syrup she'd gotten on the counter. "We'll have to wait and see. Be sure you send up a prayer to the moon goddess for her tonight, though."

"I will," I promised as the house phone rang. The sound of it startled me from my thoughts and shattered the intense moment Gran and I had been having.

I rushed to answer it. The caller ID said it was someone calling from Eddie's.

"Hello?" I asked, even though I was positive who it would be and why they'd be calling.

"Hey, Mina," a rough voice said from the other end of the line.

I reached for my keys. "Hey, Eddie. What's up?"

"How you doin', darlin'?"

"I'm okay. How about you?"

"I'm good." He sighed. "Look, I hate callin' to bother you, but your daddy is down here drunker than a skunk. Figured you'd want to know. I stopped servin' him about an hour ago hopin' he'd sober up some, but he pulled out a flask I didn't know he had and started drinkin' his own shit. I'm goin' to need someone to come pick him up."

"All right." I grabbed my purse and started for the door. Even though I was ticked Eddie had managed to over serve my dad again, I was glad he'd opted to take his keys and call him a ride. "I'll be there in a minute. Thanks, Eddie," I said before hanging up.

"I told him not to go down there and drink himself away again today," Gran insisted as she shook her head.

"It doesn't do any good. You should know that by now." I stepped to the kitchen to give her a kiss on the cheek. "Anything you need me to pick up while I'm out?"

"Actually, there is." She wiped her hands on a dish towel and grabbed a pad of paper and pen from in the junk drawer. "Let me make a short list for you."

"Okay." I leaned against the counter, watching her write.

Once she'd jotted down a list of four items total and handed me a twenty-dollar bill, I headed out the door. As a slipped in my car, I eyed Eli's parents' trailer, searching for any sign of him. Either they'd already finished their conversation, or it was still going.

I wasn't sure which would be better.

My teeth sank into my bottom lip as I cranked the engine on my car and shifted into reverse. I made a mental note to send Eli a text when I reached the grocery store, letting him know I'd learned what might be wrong with Violet from Gran and to make sure he was still alive. Would his dad do anything to him for what he'd done to Drew? Were there consequences for his action? Should I have gone with him to talk to his dad? Probably not. It was best he dealt with this on his own.

I pulled out of the trailer park, cutting a right at the entrance. It didn't take long to decide where to go first. Obviously, it would be easier to get Gran's list at the store before I picked up my dad from the bar.

That was where I headed.

4

The instant I pulled into the parking lot of the grocery store, I knew I didn't want to be there long. The whispered murmurs of Drew and what happened to him hung on everyone's lips.

That was living in a small town, though.

Having a young person die before his time, especially in an accident like Drew, was juicy gossip. No one called it gossip, but that was what it was. Everyone just called it compassionate concern in the South.

I tried to tune the talk out as I started toward the entrance of the store. How could they be standing out here in the heat chatting? Weren't they melting?

My gaze dipped to the list Gran had made as I entered the air-conditioned place. Buns, hamburger meat, sloppy joe mix, and a bagged salad. It would take barely ten minutes to get everything she needed and get out. Then I could get Dad and head home. I wouldn't have to hear any more townspeople gossip about poor Drew Hopkins and how tragic it was that he'd passed so young in such a careless accident.

It made me sick.

Didn't anyone realize how much of a monster he was? Was it possible he'd had everyone fooled?

It sure looked that way.

I grabbed some whole wheat buns from the bread aisle and made my way to the canned good section of the store for the sloppy joe mix. Tonight's dinner might not be my favorite, but it was Gracie's. Gran was making this for her. I understood. What happened to Violet had freaked her out. It wasn't something anyone thought would happen to us here in Mirror Lake.

A small group of older women stood at the end of the aisle chatting about Drew. I tried to ignore them, but their conversation floated to me as I searched for the can of sloppy Joe mix.

"His poor mama," one of them said in a voice laced with sympathy. "I can't imagine what she must be goin' through."

"Oh, I know," said another. "Having to bury a child is my worst nightmare."

"Don't you know it," the third woman said. "Remember what happened to Eloise Angel a few years back? She got so depressed after burying her little girl she nearly killed herself."

"I remember," the other two old women said in unison.

"I brought her a tuna casserole," the woman continued. "Never did get my dish back."

"Forget about your dish, Wanda," one of the other women scolded her as I squeezed past them to grab the mix.

How long would it be before the town stopped talking about Drew?

I clutched the can to my chest as I turned out of the aisle and down the next. Becca was there, studying the different types of flour. My feet faltered as guilt crept through me while I stared at her. I struggled to paint on a more neutral expression, telling myself I had nothing to be guilty for. No one suspected foul play. Everyone thought what Eli hoped they would— Drew had gotten drunk and fallen down the stairs to his basement, breaking his neck. Becca had no reason to suspect anything else, least of all anything that involved me.

She would have insight as to how Shane was handling things and what his thoughts surrounding his brother's death were, though.

I didn't care to make sure he was okay. All I wanted was to make sure he believed what everyone else did—that Drew's death had been an accident.

"Becca, hey," I said. She jumped at the sound of my voice, but still managed to turn toward me with a smile on her face.

"Oh, hey. How are you?"

"I'm good. How are you?" I asked, noting how awkward this conversation felt. Did she think so? I couldn't tell.

"I'm okay." She held up a can of bread crumbs. "Needed to pick something up for the dish I'm making Shane and his mom tonight."

She was always cooking something. Maybe it was her hobby, or maybe it was her passion; I didn't know her well enough yet to determine which.

"Speaking of Shane...how is he?"

Becca's smile slipped. "He's hanging in there as best he

can. So is his mom." Her eyes dipped to the cheap packets of pudding along the bottom shelf. "I mean, they're both taking it pretty hard—who wouldn't—but they're doing as good as they can, I guess."

"Be sure you tell him my thoughts are with him and his family," I said, hoping my words sounded sincere. That was what I supposed to say, wasn't it?

"What the fuck ever," Shane said from somewhere behind me. "You don't have any sympathy for what happened to my brother. Don't even fucking pretend."

I hadn't heard him walk up behind me, and Becca had given no indication he was there.

"I do," I said, meaning every word. While it was true I didn't care for Shane as a person, or know his mom, I still would never wish the loss of the loved one on anyone. Not even Shane.

Shane's eyes narrowed. It was clear he didn't believe a word coming out of my mouth. "You probably had something to do with it. You look like you have a guilty conscience to me."

I blinked but was unable to say anything in response. What could I say? That he was right? How could I stand here and deny I had any part in his brother's death to his face?

I couldn't. So instead, I walked away. He could take my action any way he saw fit. I didn't give a damn.

I squeezed past a mom and her three little ankle biters as I made my way out of the aisle. Hamburger meat was next on my list. Once I grabbed it, there was one more item and then I was out of here.

The bar was as bad as the grocery store when it came to gossip about Drew. Apparently he was the talk of town. The only person who wasn't discussing what happened to him was my dad. Instead he was at the bar mumbling to himself about something else. Something that probably had everything to do with my mom.

It always did.

"Well hello there, Mina," Eddie said in greeting as I entered the bar. He flashed me a gap-toothed smile as he continued to wipe off the bar top with a wet rag. "Again, I'm sorry about your dad's state of bein'. Figured I'd cut him off at the right time, but I didn't bet on him havin' his own alcohol on him."

"That's how it goes with alcoholics though, isn't it?" It was a harsh jab at my dad, and anyone else in here who suffered from alcoholism, but I couldn't hold back the words any more than I could stop my lungs from needing air to breathe.

Eddie didn't agree or disagree with what I said. Instead he continued to wipe down the bar top.

I stepped farther into the smoke-filled bar. A few of the regulars nodded and mumbled hellos my way as I started toward where my dad sat.

"Hey, Dad," I said once I reached him. "Eddie called me. He said it was time to pick you up." I patted him on the back. He jumped and then laughed.

"Mina, you scared the shit out of me," he slurred.

"Good to know," I said with heavy sarcasm. "Let's get out of here. I've got groceries in the car Gran needs for dinner tonight."

Dad stumbled, tripping on the leg of the barstool beside

his as he got to his feet. I barely caught him before he face-planted into the bar top. His cane dropped to the floor, and I bent to scoop it up while still helping him stay upright.

"What's she cooking tonight? I'm starved," he said without any indication he'd nearly wiped out as he took the cane from me.

"Sloppy joes and a salad. Gracie's favorite," I said as I steered him toward the exit. I waved to Eddie. "Thanks for the call."

"No problem. Take care, darlin'." Eddie nodded.

"Gracie, how's she doing? Haven't seen her in a couple of days I don't think," Dad slurred as I pushed open the screen door and we stepped into fresh air. I pulled in a greedy breath as we made our way to my car. I always had hated the smell of cigarettes. It clung to hair and clothes, refusing to disappear until you washed.

"She's doing fine." I didn't know what else to say. When he was hammered, he couldn't hold a real conversation anyway. Did he even realize what was going on with Violet? What about Glenn? "She'll be home tonight. She's spent the last couple of days with Callie."

"Callie Marshall?" Dad asked. His words ran together, but I could clearly make out the heavy dose of sympathy for the Marshall family etched within his tone. "It's so sad what happened to her sister. I hear you were a hero, though. The brave and beautiful Mina Beana. My girl." His hand reached out to touch my cheek, but instead he managed to poke me in the eye.

"Ouch." My eye watered as I squinted while still steering us toward my car.

Dad burst into a fit of laughter, killing the moment he'd

barely been able to create to begin with. I released a long sigh as we neared the passenger side of my car. Before I opened the door, I made sure Dad was propped against the car, knowing I would have to preform my trick with the handle before the stupid thing would unlatch. At this point I figured it would probably be cheaper to sell the clunker and buy something else than to fix everything wrong. Yes, Eli had swapped the battery out, changed the oil, and done a few other small things to it, but it didn't matter.

It was still a hunk of junk.

Once Dad was in the passenger seat, I closed the door and rounded the hood of my car. It was time to head home and see if Eli's conversation with his dad was over. I was desperate to know what they'd discussed. What our alpha thought we should do next.

I cranked the engine of my car and backed out of my parking space, ready to head home. Dad flopped around in the passenger seat as if I was going too fast and let out a groan. I prayed he didn't get sick in my car. Cleaning his puke up was the last thing I wanted to do today.

My mind drifted to Shane while I drove. Did the rest of his family think the werewolves of Mirror Lake Trailer Park had something to do with his brother's death? Or was it just Shane because he was suspicious of me?

Dad hiccuped, and I reached around to the back floorboard, searching for an unused grocery bag in case he needed to get sick. He acted as though he didn't need it and tossed it at his feet. I gripped the wheel tighter and bit my tongue.

When I reached the trailer park, I eased up on my grip. I glanced at Eli's trailer, looking for any sign he was home. No lights were on, but his truck still sat in his driveway.

"You got something going on with that Vargas boy?" Dad asked, surprising me. From the sound of his heavy breathing, I thought he'd been on the verge of falling asleep.

"No." I pulled into the parking area beside our trailer.

"I wouldn't be against it if you did," he insisted.

I grinned and rolled my eyes. "You and a lot of others."

I cut the engine on my car and climbed out. Dad fumbled with a handle on the passenger door, but he wasn't able to get it open on his own. I pressed the button and lifted up, opening the door without issue. He nearly toppled out of the car at my feet. Apparently he was more hammered than I'd given him credit for. The ride from the bar to our trailer must've allowed the alcohol to work deeper into his blood. I reached for his hands and attempted to pull him up, but he nearly pulled me down with him. I was able to right myself, and with a couple of jerks, I helped my dad to his feet.

"Come on," I huffed. "Let's get you inside."

Dad muttered something, but I couldn't make out what he'd said. I was too focused on the sight of Eli leaving his parents' trailer. My heart dropped to my stomach at the look on his face. Pissed off didn't even come close to describing it.

"Hey," I called out to him unable to stop myself. Curiosity would get the best of me if I didn't find out what they'd talked about. I needed to know if he was in trouble with his dad so I could help get him out. What Eli had done was necessary.

I understood that now.

Eli glanced at me. In the span of a single heartbeat, I noticed all of his anger leave his face. His features softened while he continued to stare at me. Maybe I was some sort of a sedative for him too. He always seemed to be one for me during tense situations.

A part of me took comfort in this thought. More than I probably should.

"Hey yourself," Eli said with a nod. A small grin quirked at the corners of his lips. "Need any help?"

I opened my mouth to say no, but before I could get the word out, my grip on my dad slipped and he fell. Laughter bubbled from his lips along with a few curse words that had me grinning like a fool. Eli was there in a flash, grabbing hold of my dad to right him.

"You know I just asked Mina if there was something going on between the two of you," Dad muttered to Eli.

"Oh yeah?" Eli asked. "And what was her answer?"

"A flat-out no." Dad chuckled. "Don't give up, though. She'll eventually cave."

Eli shifted his gaze to mine and winked. "Good to know."

I rolled my eyes. Even as I did, a wide grin sprang onto my face. Eli walked my dad to the front steps of our trailer. I slammed the passenger door of my car shut and went around to the trunk to grab the groceries I'd bought for Gran.

"The two of you have always had a strong connection," Dad muttered. "Everyone's been able to see it. Even Mina. Don't give up. She takes after her mom. Independent and stubborn as hell, but they secretly love the chase," Dad whispered as though I wasn't within hearing distance.

"I'll remember that. Thank you, sir." Eli chuckled while he reached for the trailer door.

Where the hell was all this coming from? Was it because I was spending more time with Eli lately? I knew the pack had wanted us together from the beginning. I knew I'd felt something strong toward Eli since day one. However, there was still a part of me that didn't want to give in and commit to anything with him. A part of me couldn't let go of Alec.

Was I a bitch because of it? Maybe.

I watched Eli help my dad through the front door. My mind drifted to when the last time I'd heard from Alec was. I grabbed my cell from my back pocket and pulled up our texting thread. Alec hadn't messaged me all day. He hadn't called either. I figured it was because he was spending time with Shane, helping him cope with the loss of his brother, but I'd seen Shane with Becca at the store. Alec wasn't helping him cope. She was.

Was he working?

He had gotten a job at the seed store in town, but I thought he was supposed to be off today. Sometimes he worked around the house for his parents while others he helped at the Pendergrass Farm. The thought of him hanging out with Lily irritated me. Surely, that wasn't where he was.

My thumb hovered over my keyboard as I thought of what to send him.

Hey, was just thinking about you. Figured I'd see what you're up to. - Mina

I pocketed my cell again and started to my front door.

Eli had deposited Dad in his bedroom and was making his way back down the hall. Gran stood at the stove, cooking up another concoction for Violet I was sure. I hoped one of the things she'd made would do something for her. Tether her wolf back to her. Help her heal. Something.

"Thanks for helping me with him," I said to Eli as I set the groceries on the kitchen counter.

"No problem." He nodded. I watched as he crammed his

hand into the front pocket of his cargo shorts. His gaze dipped to the linoleum floor of our kitchen, and I got the impression he had something else he wanted to say.

"Did everything go okay with your dad?" I asked even though Gran was in the room. I wouldn't press for details with her present, but he could at least answer the question with a simple yes or no.

"Yes and no," he said.

Not quite the answer I was looking for. "Okay..."

I reached for the hamburger meat and salad mix to put in the fridge.

"Want to go for a walk or something?" Eli asked as he scratched his head.

"Yeah. Sure. Let me set this in the fridge."

"Before you head out for your walk, I've got something for you," Gran said to Eli as she wiped her hands on a dish towel. She disappeared down the hall only to come back a few seconds later holding a stack of tattered and faded towels. "I was thinking the other day about things you might need besides the skillet or pots and pans and decided towels are always a good thing to have extra of." She held the stack out to him.

Embarrassment warmed my face. Gran was giving Eli our trash towels. "He doesn't need towels. He has some."

She shifted to look at me as Eli took the towels from her. "And how do you know he has towels? Have you showered there?" There was a skeptical look reflected in her eyes. Also a small sense of wonder.

I opened my mouth to say something, anything besides how I knew Eli had towels, but Eli beat me to the punch.

Thank goodness because I didn't want to tell Gran I'd seen him in nothing but one of his towels at one point.

"I do have a couple, but I agree, a person can never have too many. You never know when you might need extra," Eli said. "Thank you. They'll come in handy, considering my aversion to laundry lately."

"You're welcome," Gran said as she stepped to the stove again. "If there's anything else you need, don't hesitate to ask."

"Thanks," Eli said. His gaze shifted to me. "Ready for that walk?"

Something festered behind his eyes, giving me the impression he was eager to get whatever he and his father had spoken about off his chest.

"Yeah. Sure." I started toward the front door.

"Dinner in an hour," Gran called after me.

"Got it," I said as I exited the trailer with Eli hot on my heels.

5

We'd walked past the Bell sisters' trailer and paused to say hello before Eli finally decided to talk about what his dad had said. His eyes darkened, and I felt the first flickers of panic shift through me.

Was Eli in trouble?

"He wasn't happy with what I did," Eli said. He scratched at the back of his head with his free hand. "Apparently, there was speculation Drew's death might not have been an accident."

Alarm nipped at my insides as my heart dropped to my toes. We'd been so careful. At least I thought we had been.

We'd made sure to wipe everything off and to put things back. We'd carried Drew to the stairs and cleaned things up. Hell, we'd even burned the rags we'd used to wipe everything down. There wasn't any evidence left.

Unless...

No. The shirt I'd worn that night was stuffed in the

bottom of my clothes hamper. Besides, there wasn't any evidence on it. My blood stained it, not Drew's.

"Wait a minute, you said there *was*, as in there isn't any more?" I narrowed my eyes while I attempted to force my lungs to remember how to breathe before I had a full-blown panic attack. "Is everything smoothed over now?"

"Everything is smoothed over, but it took a little convincing from my dad's contact at the station."

I released the breath I'd been holding. "Well, thank goodness for Dan."

When we reached Eli's trailer, I started up the steps to his front door. My pulse continued to throb in my fingertips as I reached for the knob. I needed to chill out. My heart might explode if I didn't. I stepped inside his trailer and instantly froze.

Eli had purchased his first large piece of furniture—an overstuffed couch. My eyes trailed over the soft gray suede. When had he gotten this? Better yet, how had I not noticed him hauling it through the trailer park in the back of his truck?

"Aw, you're all grown up now. Look at you, you've finally got real furniture," I teased as I stepped farther inside.

A lopsided grin stretched across his face as he deposited the towels Gran had given him on the kitchen counter. "I had real furniture before. What do you call those chairs outside?"

"Bag chairs. Camping equipment. Not real furniture."

He ran a hand through his hair. "Yeah, well they were real to me."

"When did you get this?"

"I picked it up yesterday," he said. "And, yes. It does

happen to be the first piece of actual furniture I've ever bought. I guess I am all grown up now."

His eyes were on me. I could feel them, but I couldn't look at him. If I did, he might be able to see how jealous of him I was.

"That's got to be exciting." I cleared my throat, hoping to clear away my bitter emotions as easily.

It didn't work.

Instead I continued to wonder what it must feel like to live in your own place. To purchase your own furniture. To decorate with your own style. Would I ever be able to know what that felt like? Even if I was taking care of my dad?

"It is," Eli said. "It's hard, though. Took me forever to pick something out."

I crossed to the couch and skimmed my fingertips over its smooth surface. "What made you decide to get a gray one?" For whatever reason, I assumed he'd go for something black.

"Because I know you like the color."

His words surprised me. I opened my mouth to say something, but Eli spoke before I could.

"Sit. Try it out," he suggested. He stepped to the couch and flopped down, then patted the cushion beside him.

My lips quirked into a small smile as I rounded his couch to sit. It was surprisingly comfortable. The kind of couch you curl up on in a pair of comfy sweats and watch too much TV. My gaze drifted around the trailer, searching for anything else I might have missed he'd added to his space.

"The couch is all I've bought," Eli said, knowing what I was doing. A tiny wisp of unease trickled through my system at him having guessed right about my thoughts. "The towels don't count." He winked.

My gaze shifted to the stack. Gran popped into my head, and I knew I shouldn't be here much longer. One, she was cooking dinner and would have my head if I was late. And two, she probably had a mental stopwatch going since I stepped out the door. If I was here much longer, she'd begin to suspect there was more going on between Eli and me than I cared for her to.

"So," I said as I smoothed my hands along my thighs while going for a seamless topic shift but not knowing how to create one. "You said things with your dad went good and bad. I'm assuming the bad was the police suspecting foul play before Dan could change their minds."

"Sort of."

My stomach somersaulted. "What do you mean?"

"Well, maybe there was more bad than good." His teeth ground together as his jaw tightened. "My actions earned us a chaperone."

"A chaperone? Who?"

"Dorian."

"You can't be serious. Dorian is so shoved up Sheila's butt it's not even funny. How could he possibly chaperone us for anything?"

Eli cracked a smile, obviously liking my mild burst of anger. Or my valid description of Dorian. "I know, right?"

"Seriously though. Dorian isn't much older than us. I figured when you said your dad gave us a chaperone it would be someone older. Like Mr. Marshall or something."

"Nope. He chose Dorian." Eli sighed. "I'm supposed to meet with him later tonight to discuss things in-depth. Dad has filled him in on some details but not everything. Just the basics that he knew before today. He's been too busy."

"Dorian's been busy or your dad has?" I couldn't imagine what Dorian could be busy with besides sucking face with Sheila. I'd never seen a couple as all over each other as them.

"Both actually," Eli insisted. "Dorian's been helping my dad, along with Mr. Marshall and a couple others from the pack."

I leaned back against the couch, realizing whatever our alpha was dealing with must be huge if he needed to pull in so many members of the pack to help. The desire to ask for more details burned across the tip of my tongue, but I refused to let them slip free. Eli wouldn't be able to give me details anyway.

"I can see it in your eyes you're hoping for details about what my dad has been working on," Eli said.

Was I an open book to him? What the hell?

"No, I'm not." My words came out too quick to seem believable.

"Yes, you are." Eli licked his lips. "I can't tell you everything, but what I can say is that what my dad is dealing with pertains to what we're dealing with. Sort of."

He had my undivided attention.

"You know about the deal our pack has with the Caraway witches, right?" Eli asked.

"Yeah, we all know about that."

It was a simple deal. One that benefited both parties.

We kept vampires out of Mirror Lake, with the exception of the Montevallo vampire family, and the Caraway witches would keep our ceremonial grounds hidden from humans on the night of the full moon each month. It was so we could run freely and host our ceremony without risking being seen.

It was a win-win.

"Then you know the deal is no other vampires besides the Montevallo family are allowed to step foot inside Mirror Lake."

"Are you saying more have?" I asked as I held his gaze. A shiver slipped along my spine. I didn't like the idea of bloodsuckers lurking in the woods any more than I liked the idea of Shane's brothers hunting in them.

It truly seemed as though the woods of Mirror Lake were becoming more dangerous as the days passed.

Eli nodded. "A group of vampires attempted to settle in town just before Glenn went missing."

"Do you think it's a coincidence, or do you think both situations are connected to one another?" I wasn't sure I believed in coincidences, but it seemed as though that was what Eli was hinting at.

"Actually, I do think they are connected. So does my dad. We think it might have been supposed to be a distraction, but we aren't sure."

My teeth sank into my bottom lip.

"This might seem shocking to you, but my dad learned Alec's uncle is involved in some shady dealings with the new group of vampires." He paused as though allowing me to process what he'd said before pressing forward. "I know nothing I say will make you stay away from Alec, but now that I know his uncle is involved with the vampires stirring up trouble for our pack, I can't stress enough how careful you need to be while around him."

I wanted to be mad at Eli for dragging Alec into this, but I couldn't find it in myself. I knew he was only warning me again because he cared about me. On the other hand, how many times did I have to tell Eli that Alec was his own person? He wasn't his uncle.

"I get you're worried about me, but please don't play the guilty-by-association card again." The words fell from my lips before I could stop them.

"I'm not trying to, Mina," Eli insisted. His eyes darkened as his irritation toward me made itself known. My teeth ground together. If someone were to look at us right now, they'd have a hard time trying to determine who was more pissed—him or me. "All I'm saying is now that we know Alec's uncle is involved with vampires, shady vampires at that, I think you should be more careful when you're around him. I would tell you to stay away from him altogether, considering what we also know about his best—"

"You better not even go there." Anger bubbled through my system.

"I'm not saying I *am* telling you, I said I *would* tell you," Eli ground out. "There's a difference."

"I'm not sure I like you *telling* me anything. Alec is a good guy. How many times do I have to say it?" I seethed.

Eli held up his hands. "I'm not having this conversation with you. I won't argue with you either. All I'm saying is that I want you to please be careful around Alec."

I crossed my legs, folded my arms over my chest, and bounced my foot. My lips clamped shut, even though there was loads more I could say on the subject. We were never going to see eye to eye on it though so my words didn't matter.

"What are the vampires doing in town?" I asked, circling back to where the whole conversation started and getting back to the point.

"I can't give you details on that. All I can say is Alec's uncle was spotted conversing with them."

Infuriating. Eli was infuriating to me right now.

"Okay." I dragged the word out. "What's the next move? What does your dad suggest we do?"

"He agreed the next step should be checking out Peter's place, but our chaperone, Dorian, has to come with us. I've been heavily advised not to have a repeat of what happened with Drew."

I didn't want to admit it, but I agreed with Eli's dad. The worst thing we could do is allow the same thing to happen with Peter. If Peter died shortly after his brother, suspicions were sure to rise. Fingers would be pointed, and I was positive Shane would make sure most of them were aimed in our direction.

Maybe having Dorian come along was a good idea. Hopefully he had a level head in situations like this.

"Okay, so we're going to check out Peter's place," I said, leaving out how much I hoped we would find Glenn there. Getting him back to Taryn was one of my top priorities. It wouldn't completely ease the guilt I felt when thinking about his disappearance, but it would be a start.

"Didn't Drew and Shane mention something during their conversation in the woods about Peter having Glenn?" I asked.

"I think so."

"Then there's a really good chance Glenn has been at Peter's place all along." How in the hell was I just now thinking of this?

"It's possible but highly unlikely. You saw how quickly they were willing to get rid of Violet. She was supposed to be sent out the next night. If Peter did have Glenn, it's been too long since he was taken. There's no way he'd still be there. Heck, he was probably gone the day after we overheard them talking in the woods."

It wasn't what I wanted to hear. I needed some hope, damn it. "There's still a chance. You can't outright discredit my theory."

"No, I can't but I don't want to get your hopes up either," Eli insisted. "Did you talk to your Gran about Violet? Does she have an idea as to why she isn't healing properly?"

I deflated at the mention of Violet. Even if Glenn was found, there was no way in hell he'd be any better off than she was. Nausea sloshed through my stomach. He might have been severed from his wolf for good considering how long he was probably devoid of any silver.

"She has a theory, but it's not good," I said. "Gran thinks because Violet was left without silver touching her that her wolf has been severed."

"Oh shit," Eli gasped. "I didn't think of that."

"Me neither, but the bars on the cage we found her in were iron. You noticed that yourself. And she was completely naked when we found her." I chewed my bottom lip, thinking of how scared she must have felt. "She was left without silver for a couple of days. Gran says her wolf is lost. Their connection has been broken, and all we can do is pray to the moon goddess allows them to find one another again."

We lapsed into silence. I tried to imagine what it would feel like to become severed from my wolf, and Eli seemed to be equally lost in his thoughts.

"It makes sense. That could be why she hasn't healed properly yet," Eli said. He ran a hand over his face.

"Yeah, and I'm not one hundred percent sure her ankle will ever heal after this. It might be a permanent injury, something similar to what my dad struggles with." I hated it for her. It made me wish we'd gotten to her sooner. That I had done more.

I was there. I should've done something to force her back home.

It should've been me Drew took. Not her.

"Don't go down that path, Mina." Eli whispered, his words soft and sweet.

How was he doing this mind judo trick? Was it something he was doing, or had I really become that transparent with my thoughts? "What are you talking about?"

"I can see the guilt swirling through your eyes. You're feeling guilty for not getting her out of the woods fast enough. You're feeling guilty because you know Drew was there the night she was taken because he wanted you," Eli insisted. He placed a hand on my knee. I stared at it, feeling the heat from him soak through my skin. "Don't go down that path. It won't change anything, and it damn sure won't help."

"How do you do that?" I whispered.

"Do what?"

"Always know exactly what I'm thinking, what I'm feeling, without me having to say?"

"Easy." Eli grinned. His tongue snaked out to moisten his lips. "We have a strong connection, you and me."

We did. I'd felt it repeatedly over the years. Lately, the more I was around him, the harder it was to deny.

Eli's thumb made slow circles across the top of my knee as his vibrant green eyes continued to bore into me. I licked my lips and held his stare as one thought circled through my mind on repeat: Maybe it was time I let Alec go and gave into what I was feeling with Eli.

My cell chimed inside my pocket. It jolted me from the moment building between us. I stood, my heart hammering inside my chest and ran my fingers through my hair. Eli leaned against the couch and let out a sigh as though he was irritated our moment had been ruined. I started for the front door.

"I should get going." My voice shook when I spoke. "Dinner is probably ready by now. Gran won't be happy if I'm late."

"Yeah. I'm sure." Eli stood and faced me. I paused at the front door. "Well, I guess I'll talk to you later."

"Yeah, later."

I disappeared through his front door. Damn, I had a lot of thinking to do. Something big was about to happen back there. I could feel it. There was an energy in the air unlike anything I'd ever felt before. Whatever pull there was between Eli and me, it was getting stronger.

My hand gripped my cell, and I glanced at the screen to see who'd sent me a text. It was Alec.

Of course it was.

Hey. Sorry. Was working on something for my mom. We should hang out tonight.

My stomach dipped. All I could think about was how he was right—we should hang out tonight, but not for the reasons he thought.

We should hang out tonight because it was time I let him go.

6

I was nervous for my date with Alec. Normally, I was never nervous around him, but this was different. I didn't know how he would react once he learned I thought we'd be better off as friends. I hadn't dated much, and I'd never broken things off with someone before. I didn't know how this was supposed to go. What was I supposed to say?

"I don't know why you're going out with Alec again. Why even waste your time?" Gracie huffed from where she sat on the couch with Winston sleeping in her lap.

"I'm not wasting my time with him," I snapped. Since when had she become so involved in my love life?

"You are. You've been spending so much time with Eli lately. I know you like him. I can see it on your face when he's around."

I ran my fingers through my hair. "It's complicated."

"No. It's not. You either like Eli or you don't. He's the one you're supposed to be with. He's a member of the pack. Alec isn't. He never will be. It's time to let him go."

I stared at her, mouth hanging open, unbelieving how wise she sounded. As much as I hated to admit it, she was right. She knew before I did what I needed to do. Whether it was her noticing or her picking up on previous conversations I'd shared with Gran, it didn't matter.

The time had come for me to make a choice. I'd known it would happen. I just hadn't realized there would be so many people waiting for it.

Headlights flashed across the living room window as the sound of gravel crunching beneath large tires made its way to my ears.

"That's Alec," I said as I forced myself into a standing position. My knees were weak with nerves. Could Gracie tell? I shifted my gaze to her. She wasn't even looking at me. "Are you going to be okay here by yourself?"

Gran wasn't home. She was at the Marshalls' place explaining how to use the new concoctions she'd made for Violet. I wasn't sure what each was supposed to do but knew they all had something to do with calling Violet's wolf back and curbing her anxiety. She was anxiety-ridden to the max. I figured it was from a combination of not knowing if her wolf would come back and post-traumatic stress disorder from all she'd been through with Drew.

"Uh, duh. Why wouldn't I be okay here by myself? I'm thirteen, not three."

"Right. Okay. Well, I guess I'll see you later," I said as I started toward our front door. I paused and glanced back at her. "Dad's here if you need him, and Gran should be back soon."

"Yeah, like him being home even matters." She rolled her eyes. "He drank himself to sleep hours ago. Just like always."

My teeth sank into my bottom lip. I hated how she talked about him. It was the truth, but still. He was our dad. I knew Gracie deserved better, though. She deserved a dad who was sober more hours of the day than drunk. She deserved a mom who gave a shit and hadn't run away when things got hard. I wished I could give her those things, but it wasn't possible. They were all out of my control.

"I know. Love you. See you later." I slipped out the door at the same instant Alec cut off the engine of his truck.

My heart skipped a beat as I jogged down the porch steps. I couldn't believe I was contemplating breaking things off with him for good. I didn't want to hurt him.

My lips twisted into a small smile that was all for show as I climbed into the passenger side of his truck. I risked a glance at him and caught sight of the adorable grin stretched across his face.

It was then my smile became real.

My mouth grew dry. This was going to be the hardest thing I'd ever done.

"Hey," I said as I closed the passenger door.

"Hi. You look great. Thanks for letting me pick you up tonight." His lips hooked into a half grin as his eyes appraised me. Heat bloomed through my chest. I felt awful.

"You didn't give me much of a choice considering you wouldn't tell me where you're taking me." I'd tried to get his plans for tonight out of him a couple of times, but he never wavered in his decision to keep it a surprise.

I still planned to go through with letting him know I thought we were better as friends, because it needed to be done. Regardless if we'd taken separate vehicles. I could always walk home if the tension became too thick.

Alec cranked the engine of his truck. "I wanted tonight to be a proper date. Not some twenty-first century crap. Me picking you up is how it's supposed to be." His hand landed on my thigh, and he gave it a gentle squeeze. His fingertips were warm and rough from working outdoors.

Warmth worked its way through the center of my chest. I'd missed him. His touch. The sound of his voice. His soapy scent. How long had it been since we'd been in each other's presence? My mind thought back. Days. Not a week. Not a month. But it didn't stop it from feeling like an eternity.

Something about Alec called to me on a different level than what I felt with Eli. Was it possible to care for more than one guy? Alec removed his hand from my thigh and shifted into reverse. His eyes caught mine for a brief moment, and he winked. I knew then it was possible to care for two guys at once.

It didn't mean it was fair. Not to me and certainly not to either of them. This was what I'd meant when I'd told Gracie things were complicated.

I leaned against the comfortable seat of Alec's truck and listened to the lyrics of the country song softly stemming from his speakers. An important realization hit me—it was my wolf side who enjoyed being around Eli. That was the part of me that wanted him. My human side wanted Alec.

How was I supposed to choose between the two when doing so would mean choosing between the two sides of myself?

Alec turned the radio up as a new song he seemed to like came on. His hand found its way to my thigh again, and I struggled with whether I should slip out of his reach so as not to lead him on. In the end I remained still, enjoying the feel of his skin against mine one last time.

My gaze drifted out the passenger window. Where was he taking me? Rosemary's Diner? No. This wasn't the way. It wasn't the way to his uncle's property either.

When he turned down an unfamiliar dirt road, I felt my wolf's unease trickle through me. My teeth sank into my bottom lip as I struggled to figure out where we were. The headlights of Alec's truck lit up a large pond as he came to a rolling stop in front of it. The place was surrounded by woods, but they were different from the ones by the trailer park. The pond's water was still and dark. Frogs croaked and the ever-growing moon hung high in the sky.

"Where are we?" I asked as Alec cut the engine on his truck and killed the headlights.

"My second favorite place in the world."

Great. I was about to break things off with him in one of his favorite places.

I was such a bitch.

"You have two places?" I popped the passenger door open and slipped out.

"Don't you?"

I shook my head. "Nope. I only have one."

I used to have two, but I hadn't been to the second one since my mom left.

"You're allowed more than one. You know that, right?" Alec asked as he started around the front of his truck.

I laughed but didn't respond. Instead I slammed his door shut and moved to where he was.

"I wanted to take you someplace different tonight." His

tone sounded off, but I couldn't pinpoint why. "I hope that's okay. I know how much you like the woods by the lake."

"It's fine."

"Good. Stay here. Let me grab a couple of things from the back of my truck," Alec said before he walked away.

I stared out at the massive pond. My gaze drifted around. There was a small patch of woods and a never-ending field. No houses. Nothing.

Where were we? Whose property was this?

"I brought snacks," Alec said from behind me. I glanced at him from over my shoulder. He was carrying a blanket and a grocery bag. "I wasn't sure if you were hungry, but I figured it would be better to have something to eat and drink than nothing at all."

"Thanks." This was sweet. He was sweet.

He deserved better than me.

"Let me lay this blanket out and then we can sit," he insisted. "I can't stay out late tonight, but I wanted to spend time with you. A lot has been going on and a private moment tucked away with you is exactly what I needed."

Guilt slapped me. I couldn't believe I hadn't thought of how Drew's death might affect him. He probably had known him well considering how close he and Shane were.

"I'm sure. I'm sorry I haven't been there for you." I didn't know what else to say.

"It's okay," Alec said as he shifted to face me. Raw understanding shifted through his brown eyes. So, did something else. What was it? Knowing? "I get it. I wasn't implying you haven't been there for me. I've been busy, too. Making sure Shane is okay."

"Is he doing any better?"

Alec's face scrunched up as he laid out the last of the food he'd brought onto the blanket. "As good as he can be, I guess." He motioned for me to sit on the blanket, so I did. "I know you and him don't get along, but he's still my friend. Hell, we've been friends since we were little."

I picked up a strawberry from the Tupperware he'd set out and removed the green leaves from it. "I know he's your friend. And, yeah, it is true we don't get along well, but I'm still sorry for what he's going through."

"Me too." He shifted to look out at the pond. "It sucks."

"I saw him in the grocery store with Becca," I said before biting into my strawberry. "He looked awful."

"His mom and older brother don't look any better," Alec whispered. "My mom had me take over a casserole today."

"Becca said she was making something for them too when I saw her." I took another bite of my strawberry. "Why is it when someone passes everyone decides to bring them something to eat? Do people automatically think that's how everyone deals with loss? By eating their emotions away?"

Alec chuckled. "You always see things differently, don't you? Most would think people do that so the family wouldn't have to deal with cooking while going through something so traumatic."

I could feel his eyes on me, studying me.

"Sometimes. I'm sure you see things differently from others at times too." I didn't like feeling as though I was put on the spot. It had me uncomfortable in my own skin.

"Not always. Not like you." He licked his lips and swallowed hard. I caught sight of his Adam's apple bobbing with the force.

My eyes zeroed in on him, soaking in everything that was

Alec Thomas in that moment. The warmth I felt rippling from him. The sound of his breath coming faster than it had been before. The way his words seemed to tremble because of it.

Was he nervous? Excited? Anxious? Scared?

Why was he looking at me like that?

"You're different, Mina Ryan, and that's exactly what I like about you most."

All the breath left my lungs. Was he about to confess his love for me? I jerked my gaze away from his and focused on choosing another strawberry. Any other time, I might have thanked him for his words, taking it as a compliment, but not right now. Not with the way he'd said it. Not with the way he'd looked at me, or what I'd planned to do tonight.

Water splashed a few feet away, capturing my attention. I didn't see what caused the splash but saw the consequences of it disrupting the pond's water.

"A frog," Alec said.

"There seem to be a lot of those here."

"There are. Fish too. This is one of my favorite fishing ponds."

"I've never been fishing. It seems boring. I don't understand the thrill of it."

Alec grinned. "Lucky for you I brought my pole with me."

"Oh, really? Was that the plan? Get me out here so I can fish with you tonight?"

"No. I was fishing the other day and forgot to take my gear out of my truck." He stood and walked to his truck. I heard him banging around as he retrieved the pole he claimed to have. When he found it, he sat down beside me again and held it out. "Meet my oldest friend."

I laughed. "Nice to meet you."

"Stand up. Give it a try."

"I don't know how to fish. I told you," I said as I brushed my hands across my shorts.

"Well, then it's about time you learned." He motioned for me to follow him toward the edge of the pond.

Cold, damp grass tickled my feet through my sandals as I walked to where he stood. I paused at the edge of the pond a few steps behind him, and I wondered if I should be doing this. Would it lead to the right time for me to casually mention we should just be friends?

Alec held his fishing pole out to me. I took it, unsure how to hold the thing.

"Okay. Now what do I do? Shouldn't there be a worm on the end?" I asked, looking at the pole as though it was a foreign object.

"Nope. There's a lure on the end of it. Just press down on the line with your index finger, hold that little button in with your thumb, arch your arm back, and then swing it forward. Be sure you let go of the string when you try to cast it out, though."

I tried to do everything as he said it, but didn't manage to get the string to do anything besides drop right in front of us in the water.

"Yeah, it's safe to say I suck at this," I said.

"No, you don't." Alec chuckled. "It just takes practice."

I gave it one more go. The outcome was the same. If the object was to drop the line directly in front of you in the water, I was fantastic at fishing. "Whatever. Even with practice, I don't think I'll get any better at this."

Alec laughed louder. It was a rich laugh that rumbled from deep within his chest. I loved the sound of it.

"Is this what you brought me out here for? To see how much I suck at fishing so you can get a good laugh in?" I cocked my head to the side and arched a brow at him.

"No. I swear." He tried to rein in his laugh, but he was having a hard time. "I brought you out here because the woods near your place aren't safe."

A chill crept along my spine. "What do you mean they aren't safe?"

Did Alec know more than I thought he did? About the woods. About those who lived in the trailer park.

About me.

"Nothing. I didn't mean anything by it." His expression grew pinched, but not before I spotted something shifting through his eyes.

He was lying.

"But you do," I said unable to let him brush what he'd said away. I needed to know if he knew what was going on in the woods. I passed his fishing pole to him. "I can tell you're lying."

He scratched the back of his head as the ghost of a smile twitched at the corners of his lips. "I've never been good at lying."

"What's in the woods? Why aren't they safe?" He needed to stay on topic.

"Shane. He's in the woods. Patrolling."

My wolf reacted violently to the news. Shane was a loose cannon. He was too emotional. It made her nervous. Hell, it made me nervous too. He was hurting, who knew what he was capable of because of it.

"Why?" I tried to soften the expression on my face, but found it hard. "Is he blowing off steam? Is that his way of dealing with what happened to his brother?"

It was the only thing I could think of that might seem legitimate. From the look that crossed Alec's face, I knew he wasn't buying it.

"No." His eyes grew dark as his gaze locked with mine.

I licked my lips. "Then what?"

"Just...the woods aren't safe for you anymore, Mina. That's all you need to know. Okay? It's one of the reasons I brought you here tonight. This place has water. Woods. A field. It has a view of the night sky so you can see the moon clearly. It has everything your spot has, but it's safer."

Fear clenched my gut.

Alec knew. Didn't he?

"Why would I need a place that's safer?"

"You just do. Trust me, okay?" His words were caught somewhere between a plea and a demand. They sent goose bumps across my skin.

"I'm not afraid of Shane. Not unless you tell me a reason I should be." Maybe I was pushing too hard, but it was the only way I could think to get him to open up about what Shane was doing in the woods and what all he knew.

Alec tipped his head toward the sky and let out a long sigh. "Fine. Shane thinks his brother's death wasn't an accident. He thinks the werewolves, the ones in your trailer park, your pack, killed him."

My heart kick-started in my chest. The ground beneath my feet spun. How long had Alec known about me? About my pack? Did he believe we had something to do with Drew's death as well?

"That's crazy," I said. My words shaky and weak. I was attempting to deny everything, which was what I was supposed to do, but I didn't know if I had it in me. "His brother fell down the stairs, didn't he?"

"Shane doesn't believe that," Alec said.

"Do you?"

Alec swallowed hard before answering me. "No."

My wolf urged me to run, but I was frozen. My feet rooted in place as I stared into Alec's familiar chocolate brown eyes. How could I have been so blind to him? To what he knew? I'd fallen for his sweet southern charm. I'd refused to listen to any of Eli's warnings.

And now look where it had gotten me. I was in a secluded place with a human who clearly knew what I was somehow.

"I know what you're thinking. Just give me a second to explain," Alec insisted as he held up his hands in surrender. "I admitted to not believing Drew fell down the stairs and broke his neck. That's true. And, I do think your pack had something to do with his death, but I'm sure it was justified. Whatever you had to do, I have no doubt it was necessary."

I blinked. Words wouldn't form. My lungs barely knew how to breathe.

"Shane's brother Drew was not a good guy," Alec insisted. His words came out in a rush. It was almost as though he was trying to get them out as fast as he could before I bolted. "I know what they were doing on my uncle's property. Hunting. Not for rabbits or deer like they claimed but for your kind. For werewolves."

"How do you know that?" My words sounded thick.

"My uncle. I was there the day he claimed he was attacked by one of your pack."

How was that possible? The story my dad told me didn't mention anyone else being there.

"No one knew I was there. I was hiding near the edge of the lake. I'd been fishing. Until I heard shots go off. I hid behind a tree, hoping it would shield me from any stray bullets." Alec dropped his hands to his sides. He placed his fishing pole on the ground, but never took his eyes off me. "I saw a large wolf running through the woods and my uncle chasing it, shooting. By the time he ran out of bullets, the wolf was so pissed it lunged forward and bit him. I saw the way the wolf looked at him after. It wasn't normal. A normal wolf would have continued tearing into him. Hell, it would've probably killed him on the spot. But not this wolf. This wolf was different. It gave my uncle a warning and disappeared into the woods."

A wave of nausea engulfed me.

I couldn't see past the fact that Alec had known what I was all along.

"I've been coming back to the woods ever since because I wanted to see a wolf again. I wanted the experience of being around one all on my own. Maybe that's crazy, but I didn't think the wolf that day was aggressive. He wouldn't have bitten my uncle if he hadn't shot at him. I believe that." Alec took a step closer to me. I took a step back, but he reached out and smoothed a hand along my forearm. "I'm not going to hurt you, Mina. And, I hope you won't hurt me either." His brows pulled together as he struggled to gauge my reaction.

"I—"

"I never saw anything, though, each time I returned to the woods," he insisted. "Nothing besides you."

His fingers intertwined themselves through mine. His warmth seeped through my chilled skin, but it did little to calm the unease hammering through my insides. His touch felt nothing like what Eli's did. I should run, my wolf told me so, but this was Alec.

My Alec. He wouldn't hurt me. Would he?

"I noticed your connection to the moon the first time I saw you. It didn't take long to figure out you always went to the lake on a full moon to meditate. Or stare at it. Whatever it is you do." He grinned. "Even when it was daylight still, you'd go there and seek out its transparent shape. I waited for you to shift, to change, but you never did."

A recent memory of someone wearing a blue shirt watching me from the woods the night I was moon kissed flashed through my mind. Had it been Alec? Was he the one watching me? Not Shane. Not his brother. But Alec.

"I wanted to see you. The real you. I still do. You would be a beautiful wolf, Mina." Fascination festered through his words as excitement flashed behind his eyes. Alec didn't detest what I was. Instead I mesmerized him.

"Do you think someday you could let me see? Just once?" he surprised me by asking.

I swallowed hard. He wanted me to show him what I was. He wanted me to change in front of him. Wasn't this what I had wanted from him all along—acceptance? True acceptance?

Here he was, giving it to me willingly, and all I could think about was whether it was a trick. When had my mind become so dark?

When my pack members started going missing.

I looked into Alec's eyes. My wolf told me I needed to get the hell out of there, but my human side said I was staring at someone who desperately wanted to be a part of my world.

How had I missed it before? It was there in the way he looked at me. Had it always been?

I opened my mouth to say something, but a new text came through on my cell before I could.

"Sorry, it might be my sister. She's home alone tonight," I said as I fished my cell out of my back pocket. Alarm stabbed through my gut. My wolf didn't like having told him Gracie was home alone.

The text was from Eli. I shielded my phone from Alec while I read it.

I met with Dorian tonight. He wants to meet with both of us tomorrow to go over everything again and create a plan of action. Let me know what time you're available.

"Is everything okay?" Alec asked with a strong level of concern flaring through his words.

"Sort of. I think I should head home, though. Gracie is getting a little freaked." The lie rolled off my tongue. Thankfully, it must've sounded believable because Alec nodded.

"Sure. Yeah. Okay," he said. He bent down and began folding the blanket he'd laid out for us. "Listen, I know what I said tonight probably freaked you out. I'm sorry. You don't have to worry with me though. I'm not like Shane or my uncle. I don't want to hurt anyone in your pack. I don't want to hurt you. I guess... I guess I'm just fascinated your kind exists is all."

I laughed.

I didn't know why, and I damn sure didn't know how to contain it. I continued laughing like a lunatic while I stood a few feet away from him.

"What's so funny? I'm trying to apologize here." Alec chuckled.

"I'm sorry. It's just you're apologizing for freaking *me* out. Shouldn't the conversation be reversed, considering? After all, I am the werewolf."

The second the words passed from my lips I wished I could take them back. My laughing ceased as I realized I'd done the unthinkable.

I'd admitted to a human I was a werewolf.

7

As I slipped into bed that night, I couldn't believe the way my evening had turned out. The ride home with Alec had been awkward. He kept looking at me and smiling. It twisted my stomach into knots. I'd planned to tell him we were better off as friends, not admit that I was a werewolf.

How could I break things off with him now? He thought I was some fascinating mythical creature.

I tossed and turned in bed. Hours passed without me falling asleep. All I could think of was my conversation with Alec. Until I remembered what he'd said about Shane being in the woods.

Shit. How could I have forgotten about that?

I reached for my cell on my nightstand and sent Eli a text.

Are you still awake? - Mina

Seconds ticked by before he answered.

Yeah, what's up?

I chewed my bottom lip as I debated where to start. How could I fit everything into a single text?

I couldn't.

I need to talk to you. Can I come over? - Mina

It was three in the morning, but I had to get this off my chest. I had to tell Eli what I'd learned tonight. He needed to know about Shane being in the woods. The pack needed to be warned.

Sure.

I frowned at his simple response, unsure of what else I'd been expecting. I slipped out of bed, trying to be quiet. Movement in Gracie's bed caught my eye. Winston poked his head up from a mound of sheets, having seen me.

Why wasn't he in his crate? Irritation slipped through me. What was Gracie thinking? She should know he wasn't ready to be left out all night. I started toward him, ready to scoop him up and shove him into his crate, but he shifted in Gracie's arms enough that she latched onto him in her sleep. Her face snuggled against his soft fur, and I watched as he licked her cheek sweetly.

My heart melted.

I didn't have it in me to remove the little cutie from her side. The sight of them snuggling was too precious. While Gracie might be a pain sometimes, she was still cute when she was sleeping. I left them be and gathered my sandals before heading out the door.

The night air was still and thick when I stepped outside. Everything was too quiet. I folded my arms over my chest as I started toward Eli's and noticed I'd forgot to put on a bra. Maybe he wouldn't notice. My shirt wasn't tight. Then again, maybe he would.

I paused, debating on turning back for one but something shifted in the corner of my eye. An animal maybe? Whatever it was, it had my feet hustling toward Eli's place.

Braless.

The sensation of someone watching me prickled across my skin the closer to the woods I came. My imagination ran wild. Was Shane watching me, lining up his rifle as he waited for the right moment to shoot?

No. It had to be someone from the pack. There was always someone watching, wasn't there?

Nonetheless, my legs moved beneath me faster. The light in Eli's kitchen was on and so was the outside light. It illuminated his wooden stairs in a soft glow.

My sandals slapped against the wood steps as I jogged up them as though something was nipping at my ankles. The door swung open before I could knock, revealing Eli in a pair of athletic shorts that hung low on his hips.

Maybe coming over in the middle of the night wasn't the best idea.

"Everything okay?" Eli asked as he motioned for me to come inside.

I slipped past him. Icy air touched my skin. His AC must have been cranked to full blast. It was an ice box inside. I'd definitely have to ask for a sweater or blanket. There was no way I could be around him in a thin shirt with no bra in this temperature. My nipples were already hard enough to cut glass.

"Depends on what your definition of okay is," I said with a shiver. "Jesus, it's freezing in here."

"Sorry. I like to be cold while I'm sleeping," he said as he closed the door. "Want a sweater?"

"That would be great. Thanks."

Eli headed down the hall to his room, and I took it upon myself to curl up on his comfy couch. I flipped through the things I needed to say, deciding what was most important and where to start. Shane being in the woods. That was where I'd begin.

"This is the only clean one I have," Eli said as he appeared in the living room again holding a hoodie. "I wasn't joking when I said I haven't been the best at keeping up with my laundry lately."

"It's fine," I said as I took it from him. I pulled it on, equally as eager to cover up my chest as I was to be submerged in his scent.

"Are you thirsty at all?" Eli asked as he started toward the kitchen.

"I'm not drinking moonshine with you at three o'clock in the morning if that's what you're asking."

"Not what I'm asking at all." He chuckled. "I was just trying to be a good host."

Guilt simmered through me for having jumped to conclusions. "Oh. I'll take some water, please."

"That I have plenty of," Eli said as he grabbed two plastic cups from the cabinet by the sink. "So, tell me what's going on. You said you needed to talk to me?"

I smoothed my hands along my thighs. "Shane is what's going on. He's in the woods."

"What do you mean he's in the woods? Did you see him? Did he do something to you?" I didn't have to look at Eli to know his face had hardened, or that his eyes had turned a dangerous shade of green. It was clear from his tone.

"Whoa. Slow down." I held my hands up in front of me

as though they might deflect any more questions he wanted to shoot my way. "One question at a time."

Eli carried the cups of water over to the couch and handed one to me. He released a long breath. "Sorry. Okay. First question: Did he do something to you?"

"No. He didn't," I said as I took one of the cups.

Relief seemed to trickle through his features. "That's what I care about most."

His words stirred things inside me I hadn't expected to feel. I took a sip from my water to help dilute them, because now was not the time.

"To answer your other questions: No, I didn't see him. I do know he's there, though. He's supposedly guarding the woods, ready to shoot any wolf that steps inside because he suspects we had something to do with his brother's death."

"I'm not surprised. I assumed he'd feel that way and attempt to do something to retaliate," Eli said.

"I'm surprised. I worried he might suspect we had something to do with his brother's death, but I didn't think he'd stand in the woods with a gun, prepared to kill us because of his suspicions."

"You can never underestimate the enemy."

Enemy? It seemed like a loaded word. One that seemed overkill in this situation, but I guess there was truth to it. Shane was the enemy. He and his brothers had abducted pack members.

"I wouldn't expect anything less of him," Eli insisted. "My dad either. He's got a couple of the others watching over the park tonight, making sure no one heads into the woods for a quick run alone."

That must have been the eyes I felt. A small sense of comfort washed over me.

"I am curious to know how you learned Shane was in the woods," Eli said as skepticism pooled in his eyes.

He knew how I'd found out; he just wanted me to say it.

"Alec."

"Did Alec have anything else to say about the situation?" Eli asked even though it didn't seem as though he wanted to. The veins in his neck bulged at the same time his eyes darkened in color.

I thought back on my conversation with Alec. My pulse started to race. Regardless of how Eli might react, I still needed to tell him Alec knew. It didn't just involve me. It involved the safety of the pack too.

Still, it didn't mean I wanted to.

"I'm going to tell you something you're not going to like, but I need you to listen without interrupting. Okay?" I narrowed my eyes, hoping to get my point across.

A crooked grin formed on Eli's face, one that made me think he found my serious side amusing. "Yes, ma'am."

I rolled my eyes and then pulled in a deep breath before blurting my next words out. "Alec knows. About me. About you. About the pack. He knows what we are."

"Umm, most people living in Mirror Lake do," Eli said, unfazed by my revelation.

"No." I shook my head. "Most people suspect. They've heard rumors and aren't one hundred percent sure they're true, but Alec knows it's all true. He was in the woods the night your dad bit his uncle. He saw it."

Eli's brows furrowed. "No one else was there. If someone had been, my dad would've known."

"Alec was there. He was fishing at the lake when he heard the first gunshot. He hid behind a tree, worried about a stray bullet hitting him. He saw the whole thing," I insisted. "He knew there was something different about your dad's wolf. I think Alec's uncle knew the same. I think that was why his uncle started hunting us, and it's where Alec's fascination with werewolves came from."

"It's probably also why he's so into you," Eli bit out.

His words stung.

What he'd said wasn't true. Was it?

"I don't think that's the only reason he's into me, as you put it."

Eli shifted to look me in the eyes. "How can you be so blind? What does this guy have that draws you to him so damn much? Is it the fact that he's dangerous? Are you addicted to the dangerous type?"

"What? No! Alec is not the dangerous type. Besides, if I was into the dangerous type I'd be into you."

"He is dangerous though, Mina!" Eli shouted. It was the first time he'd ever raised his voice to me. I flinched at the sound of anger and authority rolling through his tone.

"I'm sorry but I don't believe that. Alec is not dangerous. His uncle, yes. He's mixed up in some dealings with shady vampires. One of his friends, yes. He's running an underground werewolf trafficking program in the woods." My voice rose as loud as his, and I didn't give a damn. "But Alec isn't a part of any of that. He's a sweet guy who happens to be fascinated by the knowledge there's something more out there than humans. The world is larger than he thought possible, and all he wants is a taste of it."

As I said this to Eli, I knew deep down how much truth

was in my words. Alec had been opened up to the world of the supernatural, and all he wanted was to learn more about it. That didn't mean he started dating me because of what he suspected I was. There was more to our relationship than ulterior motives and pretend. There was chemistry between us, which was something I didn't feel could be faked.

Eli set his cup on the floor. I watched him, noticing how tense his body had become as his irritation with me continued to grow. I set my cup down as well, thinking maybe it was time I left.

"Why are you with him?" Eli asked me point blank, his eyes never wavering from mine. "Tell me right now, after everything, why are you still with him?"

It wasn't a question I'd been prepared to answer.

"It's complicated," I said, refusing to give him anything more. I didn't need to explain myself or my love life choices to him. He was not my alpha. He held no control over me and the things I did.

"Then it's not worth it," Eli said more matter-of-factly than he had anything else tonight.

Anger lapped at my insides. "How would you know?"

"Because, when it's worth it, it's easy," he whispered just before his hands reached up to cup my face.

His lips brushed against mine in a soft, seductive way that called to the deepest, darkest places inside of me, bringing them to light before I could pull away. Everything about the kiss felt right. Everything about it felt real.

There was power in Eli's lips, a passion unlike anything I'd ever felt before.

My body responded to the feel of his lips by erasing the space between us. I melted against him. When his tongue skimmed my bottom lip, tempting me to open wider, I obeyed. My fingertips snaked across the chiseled muscles that made up his abs, marveling in the hard planes and crevices. A moan escaped his lips, fueling my sudden desire to be closer to him. One of his hands trailed down the side of my neck and then over my shoulder. His fingertips brushed along my collarbone, and I wanted them to continue in their journey along my body.

His fingers didn't listen to my desires.

Eli pulled away and pressed his forehead against mine. I listened to the sound of our heavy breathing mingling together as I struggled to figure out what the hell had just happened. My mind scolded me for giving into him, for allowing him to get so close while all my body did was crave more.

"This, us...it's not complicated," Eli whispered against my parted lips. "It's easy. It's the way it's supposed to be, Mina. Why do you keep fighting it?"

My head spun. My heart raced until it was about to explode right out of my chest. Even so, an answer formed along the tip of my tongue that held more truth than even I could handle.

"Because you only call to one side of me," I whispered. "You only call to my wolf."

Eli pulled back to look me in the eyes. "Give me a chance," he said as his fingers came up to trail along my collarbone again. When I didn't brush his touch away, his lips found their way to my neck. He kissed and sucked at my delicate skin. "I can call to your human side, too. Let me show you," he breathed against my skin.

Eli kissed along my jaw as one of his hands slipped

beneath the sweater of his I was wearing, and the thin fabric of my shirt, inching its way up my abdomen.

"I can call to both sides of you, Mina, if only you'll let me try," Eli insisted before his tongue invaded my mouth in a desperate and primal way I found intoxicating.

I allowed myself to become lost in the taste of his kiss and the feel of his touch. Nothing else seemed to exist beyond those two senses. My fingertips ran through Eli's hair, and I fought against the desire to hold his face in place. All I wanted was his lips to remain pressed against mine.

There was no denying Eli was able to call to both sides of me. I had been a fool for thinking otherwise.

Eli gripped the edge of the sweater I'd borrowed from him and lifted it over my head, breaking our kiss barely long enough for me to take it off. The thin T-shirt I had been wearing was next to go. Eli's heated stare took in every newly visible piece of me as I sat before him, naked from the waist up. While Eli had seen me naked before, it had never been in an intimate situation such as this.

This moment felt different. It was sensual and right in a way I couldn't explain. A part of me had known it would feel this way to be with Eli, though. It was small, but it grew with every tender touch across my skin and each stroke of his lips against mine. This, whatever it was between us, was larger than I was. I understood that now, same as I understood I wasn't willing to fight against it anymore. I wanted Eli. My wolf wanted Eli.

And now was the moment when we were finally going to allow ourselves to have him.

I slipped my hand beneath his waistband and felt how desperately he wanted me as well. A low rumble of a moan erupted from somewhere deep inside his chest. It amplified everything I was feeling and had me wanting to hear him make the sound again.

Eli nipped at my bottom lip, sending shivers of excitement coursing through me. I released my hold on him and pulled at his athletic shorts. They needed to come off. Now. Apparently, Eli had the same thought about the remainder of my clothing. In seconds, we were both naked. His hardness pressed against me as his mouth continued to work over mine.

"I told you I could call to both sides of you, Mina," Eli whispered as he kissed along my jaw and then down the side of my neck. His tongue snaked out to skim across my collarbone and down to my breast. A gasp escaped me. Who knew something like this could feel so good? "I knew you felt the chemistry between us. It's always been there, pulsing beneath the surface, waiting for one of us to give in and set it free. It's free tonight. Let's see where it takes us. Do you want to?"

I knew where this moment was going, same as I knew what it would mean once we were done. A pang of fear slipped through my gut, but it wasn't strong enough for me to stop what we were about to do.

"Yes. I want to," I breathed as his lips found their way to mine again.

I took charge of the kiss, giving into all of the passion and fiery sensation I felt from our connection but had pushed away for so long.

This was the moment to let go, the moment to give in. This was the moment to become one with Eli Vargas.

I closed my eyes as Eli positioned himself above me, allowing myself to focus on the two sensations that had brought us to this moment—taste and touch. As he entered me, my entire world broke apart at the seams only to be stitched together again by his tender kisses and sweet whispered nothings against my flushed skin. Eli held me in his arms strongly, lovingly, as he proceeded to brush his soul against mine. He tapped into both of my sides—human and wolf—tethering each piece of himself to me.

Warmth built through me.

It pulsed through my limbs and made everything I felt blissful. The entire moment became something beautiful. My lips curved into a small smile as ecstasy enveloped me. Eli was leaving his mark on my soul, on my wolf, and I was doing the same to him.

The two of us were imprinting.

After this moment, nothing would ever be the same between us. It would be right. It would be beautiful. But it would never be the same.

I pressed my lips against his and moved them in a slow, loving way that mimicked how he'd kissed me seconds before. Our breath mingled and our skin continued to touch in places it never had. The warmth I felt building reached its peak, causing my limbs and muscles to feel languid. Eli had worked his way into every cell of my being. There wasn't a single part of me that his reach didn't touch.

It even trumped the places where I thought Alec would always remain.

I realized then that Alec had been a distraction. From Eli. From the looming full moon. From my fear of never becoming moon kissed. From not having been able to help Glenn like I thought I should.

Alec had been a distraction from my *other* life—my pack life.

I knew this with a certainty. Even if it did make me seem cruel. He'd never been the one for me; it had always been Eli that I belonged with.

8

Sunlight irritated my eyes. I rolled around in bed until I found a dark spot. All I wanted to do was sleep, but I couldn't find a comfortable position. Irritation pulsed through me as I sat up in bed.

Oh shit. This wasn't my bed. Where was I?

I glanced around, taking in the sparse decor and dirty clothes tossed all over. This was Eli's bedroom. I was still in his trailer. Memories of last night came rushing back. Eli and me. Skin against skin. Hot kisses and tender touches. Our souls connecting.

Us imprinting with one another.

Eli was mine, and I was now his. Forever.

Delicious tingles slipped up and down my spine as everything about our beautiful moment together flooded my senses...until I remembered Alec.

I had to let him know about Eli and me. He needed to be told today. It was cruel of me to continue stringing him along.

Maybe it always had been, but I'd found reasons to make it all seem okay. Good enough reasons for me to believe them.

Now, there wasn't a single reason. Alec deserved to know about Eli and me. I owed him that much.

I smoothed a hand over my face. Where was Eli? And how did I end up in his bed? The bits and pieces I remembered from last night didn't involve a bed. They involved a comfy couch I'd never be able to look at the same way again.

I glanced around Eli's room. The sheets were crumpled beside me as though someone had left them recently. Had he gotten up to use the restroom or for a sip of water? What was I supposed to do? Stay where I was until he came back?

I pulled my knees up to my chin as I thought about the only other time I'd been in his room. I remembered wondering then what it would be like to sleep with Eli, but I'd been quick to push the thought away. My lips quirked into a smile because it seemed silly to push any thoughts of Eli away now.

A noise captured my attention. I silenced my racing thoughts as I focused on the sound and moved to the edge of the bed. Eli was close. I could feel him. His presence was strong, and the magnetic pull I'd felt toward him had intensified tenfold since last night. He was a part of me now.

"I know you're awake," Eli shouted. Was he in the kitchen? "I can hear you wiggling around in the bed. Come to the kitchen and eat. I made us breakfast."

I arched a brow. Eli had cooked?

"I'm coming," I said as I slipped out of bed. It was then I realized I was still naked. While I'd love to walk into Eli's kitchen in my birthday suit and surprise the hell out of him, he didn't have mini-blinds on his windows. There was no way I wanted to give Mr. Russell a show this morning.

"Hearing you say those words will never grow old," Eli called out to me. I didn't have to see his face to know a grin was hanging on it.

"I'm sure," I said as I scanned his bedroom floor, searching for my clothes.

They weren't in here. All I saw were Eli's discarded dirty clothes. He wasn't kidding when he said he'd had an aversion to laundry lately. From the piles scattered across his floor, I wondered if he knew how to use a washer and dryer.

A folded T-shirt on top of his dresser caught my eye. I wasn't sure if he'd set it out for me or if it was the last clean article of clothing he owned, but I picked it up and slipped it on. Eli's scent—masculine and musky with a hint of woods—floated to my nose, sending a sense of comfort to wash over me. I was home again.

The thought jolted me. When had Eli become home?

My guess was last night, but as I thought about it, I realized somewhere deep inside there had always been a piece of him that made me think of home. Last night had only made it come to full bloom.

I left his bedroom and started down the hall. The scent of something peppery lingered heavily in the air. He definitely wasn't cooking macaroni and cheese for breakfast.

"What are you cooking?" I asked as I stepped into the open living room and kitchen area. When I reached him, I wrapped my arms around his waist and pressed my face against his bare skin. The only thing he had on were the athletic shorts I remembered from last night. I placed a kiss to his skin and then glanced over his shoulder to see what he was cooking. A piece of bread with an egg sunny side up sizzled in the hot pan. "What's that?"

"An egg in a basket," Eli said. "Haven't you ever had one before?"

"No, I can't say that I have." I released my grip on him and moved to lean against the counter. "Do you have any juice?"

"I have coffee," Eli said as he placed a kiss to my temple. My heart pounded in a needful rhythm wanting more of his lips on me.

"I don't drink coffee," I admitted. "I've never been able to get over the taste. It's always bitter. No matter how much sugar or cream I dump in it."

"I'll have to remember that." He flipped the piece of bread with the egg nestled inside over. "I'll get juice for the next time you spend the night."

"Who said there'd be a next time?" I asked as I shifted to face him fully. His arm snaked out, and he pulled me into him.

"Me." His lips brushed against mine, causing my knees to grow weak. I pulled away, breaking our kiss all too soon because all I could think about was how horrible my morning breath probably was. Eli trailed his lips along the side of my neck, unfazed by my reluctance to kiss him first thing in the morning. "And your body. It's definitely telling me there will be a next time."

Damn him.

"Are you ready for a repeat of last night?" he asked. His voice had grown low and husky. Sexy.

I opened my mouth to say yes, but my stomach grumbled painfully loud.

"Umm, I think I need breakfast first," I said as my lips curved into a slight smile.

"Which is why I got up to make you something." He released me and went back to his abandoned pan.

"How did I end up in your bed last night?" I asked as I hoisted myself on the counter beside where he was cooking. "I don't remember walking back there at all. The last thing I remember was the couch." It was amazing how the words could come out of my mouth without my cheeks heating from the topic of conversation.

"I carried you," he said with a shrug of his shoulder as though it wasn't a big deal. "I wanted to make sure you were comfortable while you slept."

"Aw, that was sweet of you."

"I know." He grinned. "Did you sleep well?"

"I did." In fact, it was the most peaceful sleep I'd had in forever.

"I did too." He reached into the cabinet beside the stove and grabbed two paper plates. "All right, breakfast is done if you want to grab a fork."

I slipped off the counter and stepped to the silverware drawer to grab us each one. Eli handed me a plate, and I handed him a fork before hoisting myself back up onto the counter to eat. The entire exchange of silverware and food seemed incredibly domesticated, yet it felt normal to be having breakfast with him in his place.

It was amazing how things could change so quickly. If someone had told me a month ago I would be wearing only a T-shirt while sitting on Eli Vargas's kitchen counter, eating breakfast with him, I would've told them to go home because they were drunk.

"When are you going to get a dining room table?" I asked as I debated how to eat the egg thing he'd made.

"Probably not for a while," Eli said. I watched as he stabbed his fork into the center of the yolk, busting it. He cut the corner of the bread off and then dipped it in the yoke. "You could always sit on the couch if you wanted."

"No way. That couch is not for eating on."

"And why is that? You don't like to mix pleasure with food?" He arched a brow.

"No. It's just too pretty," I said as I mimicked what he'd done with his yolk and bread. "I wouldn't want it to get dirty. I can be a messy eater." As I said this, a drop of yolk dripped from my fork and landed on the front of his shirt I was wearing.

"I can see that." He chuckled. "I'll try to get us a table, then."

Us? Had he really said *us* with the implication we were living together? Or had he meant for when I came over to eat with him again?

"Don't look so scared. I'm not asking you to move in with me...yet." He grinned. "But you have to know it will come eventually. You'll get tired of sleeping alone at your Gran's, and you'll be begging me for a key to my place."

I glared at him. He was so sure of himself it was almost comical. "You really think that's what will happen?"

"Oh, I'm positive." He winked.

"Want to make a bet?"

"I'm not really the betting type of guy, but in this situation, I might be." He licked his lips, and it was all I could do to not lean forward and kiss him. "Give me the details of the bet."

I thought for a second before answering, trying to come up with something good. Nothing fantastic came to mind, so I went with the first thing I thought of instead. “Okay, if you ask me to move in first, I get to repaint this place in colors of my choice.”

“Okay,” he said with a slight nod. “What if you ask me first if you can move in?”

“Umm, don’t you think you should get to decide what you get? I don’t think you understand how this works,” I said with a chuckle.

“Oh, I understand. I just thought you wanted to be the one setting both wagers.”

“Nope, fair is fair. I set mine, now you set yours.”

“All right, if you ask me if you can move in before I ask you, then I get tomato soup and grilled cheese at least once a week made by you...*naked*.”

Of course, he would turn this into something sexual. He was a guy, after all.

While I wasn’t big on cooking, I thought I could handle his wager. “Deal.”

I held my hand out so we could shake on it.

Eli gripped my hand in his. “I think I like this betting thing, especially when it involves you.”

“Don’t look so smug. You haven’t won anything yet.”

“Yet being the operative word.” He winked as he let go of my hand and picked up his fork again.

We finished our breakfast in silence, but it was a comfortable silence. I imagined Eli was thinking of his betting terms. I was sure it was obvious I was thinking of mine.

In my head, I was repainting the walls of his trailer,

searching for a color that might fit with his beautiful gray couch.

"I should get going." I tossed my paper plate in the trash and my fork in the sink once I'd finished my egg in a basket, which happened to be delicious. It was such a simple breakfast, but so good. "I'm sure Gran is wondering where I'm at. Gracie, too."

"They won't care you've been away once you tell them you were with me." A smug sense of satisfaction dripped from his words.

"You're probably right, but I still need to head home."

Eli tossed his paper plate in the trash and started for the sink. After he chucked his fork in it, he reached for me. His arms wrapped around my waist as he pulled me close. I licked my lips in anticipation of his kiss, knowing one was coming.

"I wish you'd stay, but I understand," he said.

"Is this you wishing I'd *move in*?"

His eyes twinkled as a wide smile spread across his face. "I'm not asking you to move in. I'm asking you to stay longer," he clarified.

"Okay, just checking," I said before brushing my lips against his.

Eli took control of our kiss. His lips worked over mine in the fiery way they had the night before and lust sparked to life inside me.

Holy hell, becoming imprinted had definitely intensified things between us. Like times one hundred.

Eli pulled away all too soon. "I guess I'll let you head home. Remember though, we're meeting with Dorian at noon to go over the game plan so we're all on the same page before heading to Peter's house today."

The mention of Dorian and Peter killed the moment for me. It also reminded me of what today was—Drew's funeral.

"Yeah, I remember," I muttered as I headed to the couch to gather my clothes.

Once I grabbed them, I went to the bathroom and changed.

"You didn't have to change," Eli said as I emerged from his bathroom. "I liked the sight of you in my shirt."

"I'm sure you did." I held the shirt out to him. "But I think this is the only clean article of clothing you own, and it's not even clean now that I dripped yoke on it."

A wicked grin twisted across his face. "You're probably right about that. I need to figure out this whole laundry business."

"Laundry 101, coming up." I headed back to his bedroom. Eli followed me.

"What are you doing?" he asked as he watched me from the doorway while I buzzed around his bedroom, scooping up his dark clothing first.

"Gathering a load of laundry so I can teach you how to use your washing machine." I glanced at him from over my shoulder. "You do have laundry detergent, right?"

"Yeah. My mom gave me some as part of her moving out present."

"That was sweet of her," I said as I picked a few more dark articles of clothing off the floor. "Here, take these to the washer." I handed him the clothes I'd been holding and then bent at the waist to grab a few more dark T-shirts.

I started down the hall and spotted Eli at the washing

machine off the kitchen. He lifted the lid and crammed his clothes inside. At least he had enough sense to spread them around instead of keeping them lumped in one spot. There was hope for him yet.

"Okay, so here's what you do first," I said as I tossed the clothes I held into the washer as well. "Gather clothes, place them in the washing machine, pour a quarter cup of detergent in, close the lid, and press this button. Done. Wasn't so hard, was it?"

"Why did you grab all the dark clothes? Do they really have to be separated like that?"

"If you want your colors to keep their colors, then yes. Don't ever wash whites with darks. You'll end up with a mess. Trust me." I'd learned that the hard way last summer when I ruined my favorite pair of white shorts.

"What about lights and darks? Can those be mixed?"

"No. Not unless you want faded colors quick. At least that's what Gran says." I looked through the cabinet above his washer and dryer, searching for dryer sheets. A box of them caught my eye. Thankfully, his mom had given him everything he needed to do his laundry. "Once the machine goes off, you move all of the wet clothes into the dryer and put one of the sheets in. Clean the lint trap. Press this button and voilà, clean clothes."

"Sounds easy enough. Thanks for the lesson." Eli smirked as he pulled me into him again.

"You're welcome." I brushed my lips across his. "I need to go, though."

The longer I stayed, the more awkward it would be when I walked in the door at Gran's.

"I'll see you at noon," Eli said as his fingertips dug into

my hips. It made him seem unwilling to let me go. I loved that.

"Noon. Got it. Are we meeting here?"

"Yeah."

"You better have lunch waiting then." I slipped out of his grasp and headed for his front door. "A grilled cheese would be nice. It would be even better with tomato soup, though."

"Hey, you're the grilled cheese master. Not me."

"You were there when I cooked them last time. You know my method. See you at lunch," I said as I slipped out the door.

I wasn't expecting him to cook me a grilled cheese with tomato soup; I was only teasing. However, it would be a nice gesture if he did.

Gravel crunched beneath my sandals as I started toward Gran's trailer. I had no idea what time it was, but I knew the sun was growing higher in the sky by the second and the slight chill that always seemed to dampen the air on summer mornings had already started to dissipate.

The clanking of a glass caught my attention as I neared the Bell sisters' trailer. I cringed as I spotted them on their porch, sipping a yellowish-orange liquid out of champagne flutes.

"Good morning to you, Mina," the oldest Bell sister said.

I plastered a smile on my face and wondered if I'd be able to play it off as though I'd come from a walk at the lake instead of Eli's. Probably not. The sisters would most likely smell Eli on me.

"Coming from Eli's so early in the morning, are you?" the youngest of the Bell sisters asked. Her knowing tone made my heart beat out of its normal rhythm.

It wasn't that I was embarrassed to have been caught leaving Eli's trailer early in the morning, I just didn't like the way she was looking at me. All smug and condescending.

I opened my mouth to say something in response, but caught sight of Gran carrying groceries into our trailer. "Looks like Gran just got back from the store. I should help her carry the groceries in. Have a good morning, ladies."

I rushed toward Gran, not caring if she noticed I was coming from Eli's after having spent the night, talking with her about it would be better than talking with the Bell sisters.

"Morning," I said as I walked up to her and reached into the bed of my dad's truck for the remaining groceries bags. "Let me help you carry these inside."

"Thank you." Gran stared at me. Her eyes soaked in every inch of me. Would she be able to spot something different? Would she know something had changed? "I thought I heard someone leave last night around three. Was that you?"

"Yeah. It was me. I couldn't sleep," I said without meeting her eyes.

"And you're just now getting home?" She turned toward the trailer to start up the stairs. Was she really doing this? Was she really going to make me say I'd been with Eli?

"Yeah. I went to Eli's to talk to him but ended up staying the night," I admitted, trying to make myself sound as though it wasn't a big deal.

Gran glanced at me from over her shoulder. "Oh. Okay."

She opened the door and stepped inside without another word. I didn't know what I'd expected her to say, but that wasn't it.

"Okay? That's all you have to say?" I asked as I followed her through the door. I closed it behind me with my foot.

"What more do you want me to say? I'm sure you don't want to go into details about your night with Eli. Do you?"

"No, but I figured you'd have something else to say besides *okay*."

"Like what?" Gran asked as she set the groceries on the counter.

"I don't know," I said as I placed the bags I'd carried inside beside hers and tossed my hands up. "Maybe I told you so. Maybe I'm glad you finally gave Eli a chance. Maybe the two of you were destined to end up together or some other woo-woo response. Anything besides just okay."

Gran shifted around to face me. She placed her hands on my shoulders and looked me directly in the eye. "I'm glad you finally gave Eli a chance. I always knew the two of you were destined to be together. The heart wants what the heart wants. I'm glad you finally gave your stubborn side the boot where it concerns him."

I laughed and rolled my eyes.

"There, now that's out of the way, why don't you put these groceries up?" Gran insisted. "You might want to take a shower afterward because you reek of Eli, which is something I don't think your father will want to wake up smelling on you."

I pursed my lips together. Yeah, that might not be the best idea. While I knew he would find out Eli and I had imprinted soon enough, I didn't think he'd enjoy learning about it within the first two minutes of waking.

I rushed to put the groceries up and then hightailed it to the shower.

9

After a long shower, I headed to the kitchen for a glass of water. My cell rang before I made it, and I backtracked to my bedroom to grab it off my dresser where I'd left it charging. Alec's name lit my screen. Dread pooled in my stomach at the sight. I didn't want to answer his call, but I knew I needed to. Especially after what we'd talked about last night and what happened between Eli and me.

I always thought I would never be cruel enough to break up with someone over the phone, but here I was, contemplating taking the easy way out while I stared at his name lighting the screen of my cell.

"Hey," I said when I answered.

"Morning. I didn't wake you, did I?" Alec asked.

"No. I've been up for hours."

"Oh, okay. I was worried you'd still be sleeping. I don't know what time you normally get up in the morning. It's not something we've ever discussed—whether you're a morning person or a night owl. I always assumed you were a night owl, because of...well, you know." He fumbled his words a couple of times, but kept going.

It was clear I wasn't the only one nervous during this phone call.

"I don't have a preference, actually. I'm not either. I like to think I'm somewhere in the middle, I guess," I said.

"That's good." He released a long breath. "Look, I couldn't sleep last night because of everything I said on our date. I kept thinking about how I must've sounded... like I was only with you because of what you are and not because of who you are. I wanted you to know that's not true. Not at all."

Why did he have to be so damn sweet?

Imprinting with Eli and breaking things off with Alec couldn't have come at a worse time. There was no way for me to not make it seem as though I was breaking up with him because he knew what I was. There was no way to not break his heart, but there was also no way I could continue letting him think we were dating when I'd already given myself fully to someone else.

"Thanks, but umm, there's something I have to tell you," I said as I closed my eyes, forcefully pushing the words past my lips.

"You're breaking up with me, aren't you?" Alec asked with a sigh. "I knew it would happen."

My mouth grew dry. I licked my lips and picked my next words carefully. "It has nothing to do with you knowing what I am."

"You don't have to explain. Or lie. It's okay. I didn't think we'd last long anyway. I've always thought of our relationship as temporary."

Was he joking? How was he was handling this so well?

It wasn't as though I expected him to become irate and start calling me names, but I damn sure didn't expect him to say he knew it would happen, that he'd thought of our relationship as temporary.

"Why would you think that?" I asked, curiosity getting the best of me.

"I'm not a werewolf. I'm not like you. Things with us would never last or become long term, right? I mean, it seems like everyone in your trailer park is a werewolf. Unless you made me into one, I don't see us being able to be together forever. It would break one of your pack laws or something, wouldn't it?"

His words broke my heart, but he was right.

"I can't make you into a werewolf. It's something you're either born with or you're not. It's not like in the movies were someone gets bit and turns into a werewolf at the next full moon."

"I know that much, but only because I thought it would happen to my uncle. It never did. All it left behind was a scar. That's how I figured out everything I'd seen on TV about your kind was probably a myth."

My teeth sank into my bottom lip. He was too smart for his own good.

"I'm sorry." I didn't know what else to say. This was the weirdest break-up to ever go down in history.

"You don't have to be sorry. I knew this was coming, remember? We're good. At least on my end. Are we good on yours too? I don't want you to disappear on me." He chuckled.

"I'm not going anywhere. You don't have to worry."

"Good," Alec said. "You wouldn't only hurt my feelings if you disappeared, you'd hurt everyone else's feelings too. Benji's especially. He really likes you."

"I like him too." I smiled even though he couldn't see me. "Except for when he has all that black crap stuck in his teeth."

"I know. No one likes that," Alec said.

Silence built between us. I didn't know how to go about wording the next thing I needed to tell him.

"We're heading to the track later to blow off some steam since today is Drew's funeral," Alec said before I could speak again. "Did you decide if you were coming to pay your respects? It's at one."

"I don't think it would be wise of me to come." Shane didn't want me there, and frankly, I didn't want to be there.

"You're probably right," Alec muttered, and I wondered what Shane had told him. Did Alec think I had anything to do with Drew's death? "If you're not doing anything around four, I'd love it if you headed out to the track to ride four wheelers with Benji and me. I doubt Shane will be there. He'll probably be spending time with his mom and oldest brother. Becca will be out there later tonight, Ridley too. If you don't feel like it though, I totally understand. I just wanted you to know that's what we're all doing. I don't want things between us to be weird."

"I can't make any promises about tonight, but it's something I'll keep in mind." It felt like an honest answer, even though deep down I knew it wasn't. I wouldn't be going out to the track tonight because I had no idea how scoping out Peter's house might go. "I have something pack related I'm supposed to do. Also, I have to be honest with you about something else. You might not want me coming to hangout after you hear what else I have to say."

"You're with that Vargas boy, aren't you?"

How did he know that? A shiver crept up my spine as I wondered if he'd somehow saw me heading to Eli's last night.

"I am."

"Figured. I saw the two of you in the woods a few weeks ago at the last full moon. I couldn't hear everything you were saying, but I did manage to catch a word here and there. He said something about some sisters knowing he would be lying. I didn't understand it, but it didn't matter. All that mattered was the way you looked at each other. There's something strong between the two of you, and it's easy to see that it's a lot stronger than anything we ever had."

How did he pick up on so much in such a small chunk of time? The moment he was talking about had only lasted a few minutes before Eli walked away. The memory of how much I'd wanted him to go to the lake with me shifted through my mind, causing a yearning to be near him to sweep through me. I shoved the sensation away.

"I swear to you I'm not as much of a stalker as I sound like I am. I was in the woods close to where you were that night and saw the two of you together. I knew then that I'd been right and what we had wasn't going to last. I've been waiting for you to let me down easy ever since."

I didn't know what to say. Alec had been dropping bombs on me lately left and right, but this one blew me right out of the water. "Yeah, I'm not going to lie and say you're not freaking me out."

"I'm sorry. I don't mean to. Trust me, that's not what I'm going for."

"Okay," I said.

"Okay?"

"Yeah. You asked me to trust you. Considering everything I was keeping from you, I think I at least owe you that. You're right. There is something larger than life going on with Eli and me."

"Like you're fated to be mates?" he asked.

"Yuck. I hate that word."

"Fated?"

"No, mates." It left a bad taste in my mouth just saying it.

"Why? Isn't that what your kind calls it?"

"Not always. Some do, but we choose to call it imprinting in our pack."

"Okay, so the two of you are imprinted then. I guess, congratulations."

The sadness to his words tugged at my heartstrings. This conversation had grown past awkward. It was time to nip it in the bud.

"Right. Listen, tell Shane I'm sorry for his loss at the funeral today. I'm not going to make you any promises about tonight and four-wheeling, but thanks for the invite," I said, hoping he caught on that I needed to get off the phone.

"I will." He cleared his throat. "I guess I'll just say I'll see you when I see you."

"That works," I said. "And thanks for being so cool about everything."

"You don't have to thank me. It just is what it is."

"Bye," I said before I hung up.

I leaned against my dresser and replayed the entire conversation in my head. Alec had known about Eli and me. He'd seen us in the woods, and he'd never said a word to me about it until now.

Maybe Eli had been right. Maybe I did need to be more cautious when I was around Alec. There seemed to be a lot about him I'd underestimated.

10

I felt like all eyes were on me as I walked from my place to Eli's at a little before noon. Eli's mom was outside tending to her flower bed, but I swore she stared at me from the corner of her eye. The Bell sisters were on their porch still, their orange drinks replaced with something a translucent yellow. They smiled and waved as their eyes continued to follow me to Eli's. Even Mr. Russell sat in a chair outside beneath the shade tree at the corner of his trailer. In his lap was a gun he appeared to be cleaning. I could feel his eyes on me, though.

The news of Eli and I imprinting had spread through the park like wildfire.

Could the others sense it? Was that why they were all staring? Or was I being paranoid? Had everything about Alec freaked me out so badly that now I questioned every person's intentions within a five-mile radius around me?

I stepped to Eli's front door and knocked, anxious to get inside and out of everyone's view.

"You don't have to knock anymore, Mina," Eli shouted from somewhere inside. "Come on in. Mi casa es su casa."

My lips cracked into a tiny grin as I opened the door and stepped inside. "Since when do you speak Spanish?"

Eli was in his living room, setting up a large flat screen TV. The box it had come in was tossed on the floor beside him, along with all the paperwork and packaging.

"That Spanish phrase is about as basic as they come. Who doesn't know what it means? I mean really?" He shook his head.

"Nice TV," I said as I crossed the trailer to where he was, my arms folded over my chest. "Trying to make this place more livable to entice me to ask if I can move in?"

"No. I'm just tired of staring at my tiny cell phone screen every time I want to watch something," Eli said as he hoisted the TV up to lock into the brackets he'd secured to the wall. He took a step back to glance at it. Once he adjusted it a little, he bent down for the remote on the floor. "But, if it helps entice you to ask to move in with me, then so be it." He grinned as he scooped up a couple batteries and placed them in the back of the remote.

"I don't watch much TV, but it is something," I said.

Eli's place was starting to come together. I was glad I'd been able to see it from the beginning.

"I don't watch much TV either, but when I get the hankering to, I want to see it on something larger than four inches."

"Did you just say hankering?" My eyes bugged a little. "Wow, way to sound like a true hick."

"I thought you liked a guy with a southern drawl."

Was that a jab at Alec? I didn't get the impression Eli was

trying to start something with me. Maybe I was looking into things too closely. I decided to let it go. Today was not the day to be at odds with one another. There were more important things to think about—like rescuing Glenn.

I pulled out my cell and glanced at the time. "I thought you said noon. It's ten after twelve. Where is Dorian?"

"He'll be here." As soon as Eli said the words, there was a hard knock at the door. "See? What did I tell you?"

Eli passed me the remote to the TV as he started for the door. I held it but didn't push any buttons. I knew nothing about programming things.

"Come on in," Eli said as he opened the door for Dorian.

Dorian stepped inside dressed in a black T-shirt, dark blue jeans, and a pair of scuffed up biker boots. A no bullshit attitude surrounded him. I'd never hung around Dorian much. All I really knew about him was that he was always dead serious, except for when he was with Sheila. That was the only time he seemed to let down his walls and relax. He was three years older than Eli, and he was a born member of the pack. Not some transplant or rogue who decided he liked our pack more than his original. His parents lived in the trailer behind Felicia's. He also had a brother a year older than I was who lived with them still.

"Good, I'm glad you're here already," Dorian said as he eyed me. "We're short on time, and we have a lot to discuss."

How were we short on time? It was barely after twelve. Drew's funeral wasn't until one. The service would last about an hour. That would be plenty of time to find Glenn and get the hell out of there. Also, what was there left to discuss? Eli had told him everything already.

"I need you to recount everything from the beginning for me," Dorian insisted as his wild blue eyes fixed on me.

"Why? Eli already told you everything." What would be the point of me rehashing all of the details for him again? To me, it seemed like a waste of time.

Irritation sparked through Dorian's eyes. "There are two sides to every story. I've heard Eli's. Now I want to hear yours."

He was serious and a little intimidating, to be honest.

I'd always known he was a somber guy, but I hadn't realized it went to this level. He obviously took his job seriously. That was a good thing, considering he worked with the alpha closely. Dorian's dad was the alpha's second-in-command. Two thoughts hit me at once the instant I remembered this: One, I knew way more about Dorian then I thought I did. And two, it shouldn't have been a surprise Mr. Vargas had chosen Dorian to be Eli's chaperone.

Actually, it was a good play on our alpha's part now that I thought about it. A new generation of leader and second-in-command working together on something pack related.

"Fine. I was walking home with someone the night this all started, and I happened to hear someone from the pack in the woods."

"What do you mean you heard someone from the pack? Can you be specific?" Dorian asked.

I fought the urge to roll my eyes. "I heard a wolf let out a crazy howl. It sounded as though they were panicking," I said, trying to think back on whether there was anything I was missing. Under Dorian's intense gaze, I felt as though I was on trial.

"That's not everything though, is it? You're leaving out

one key factor," Dorian said. There was a wild note whirling in the pitch of his voice. It caused my chest to tighten.

"And what would that be?" I asked as I refused to let myself look away from him.

"Who you were in the woods with and why."

My gaze shifted to Eli. I didn't want to mention Alec in front of him, but only because I assumed it might stir up emotions now that we were imprinted I'd rather he didn't have to feel.

It looked as though Dorian wasn't going to give me an option, though.

"I was with Alec Thomas. He was walking me home from a date that night." The words burned my tongue. I continued to stare at Eli, waiting to see his reaction to the reminder of me with someone else.

He didn't have one.

In fact, he flashed me a crooked grin and nodded his head as though he knew of my internal battle and was telling me everything was okay.

God, he was sexy.

"Continue," Dorian prompted.

"Right, umm. I went back to the woods the next day to go four-wheeling with Alec and a few of his friends. When I went to use the restroom behind a tree, I noticed some blood on the ground in an area where it looked like a struggle had taken place. I immediately thought to check the pack and see if anyone was missing or hurt because I related what I was seeing to what I had heard the night before."

"Was anyone hurt or missing?" Dorian asked. I hated the tone he'd used. It sounded slightly condescending and rubbed me the wrong way.

"You know as well as I do Glenn was missing," I said, holding his gaze. Everything about this conversation was getting on my nerves now.

"How did you come to that conclusion, though?" Dorian asked as he folded his arms across his wide chest.

I released a breath of air and rolled my eyes. "Everyone knew Glenn was missing. Taryn had told everyone. The alpha. The police. All of their friends. Neighbors."

"Did you speak with her? Did you ask her anything pertaining to Glenn's disappearance?"

Was I on trial? Did Dorian think I had something to do with Glenn's disappearance? With Violet?

"Yeah, I talked to her. That was how I put two and two together and realized it was Glenn I'd heard howling in the woods."

"Did you say anything to her about what you heard or what you thought?"

"No."

"Why not?"

Guilt swam through me. My cheeks heated and the tips of my ears burned. "I didn't know if I should. I didn't know if I was right. I was afraid to upset her any more than she already was. There were loads of reasons why I didn't say anything to her."

"Okay, I think you've heard enough," Eli said, interrupting the exchange happening between Dorian and me. "You know the beginning from her and the rest of it from me. I think it's time we move on. Like you said, we're short on time."

"Fine. We can go from here," Dorian agreed. He leaned against the kitchen counter, his arms still folded across his chest, and crossed his legs at the ankles. "Here's the plan. While Peter and his family are at Drew's funeral, we're going to his house to scope it out. We need to figure out how many possible exits and entry points there are, if there are any neighbors close by, if there's a basement or garage, even a shed. We also need to know if he has any animals." He ticked each thing off his fingers.

Dorian's plan was thorough, that much was for sure, but it also seemed too time-consuming. Eli and I hadn't done any of those things when we went to Drew's house. I didn't remember caring if he had pets or where each exit was while we were circling his house in the dark. I guess I was all about the action. The only thing on Dorian's list I'd paused to think about was if Drew had any neighbors close. Other than that, all I had wanted to do was barge in and see if Violet was inside.

"We're not entering his house today. All we're doing is a little recon," Dorian insisted as his eyes bounced between Eli and me.

"You can't be serious. As much as I hate that we're snooping around his house while he's at his brother's funeral of all things, we couldn't ask for a better time to get inside and see if Glenn is there." I glanced at Eli, hoping he was seeing reason. "Right?"

Eli nodded. "Yeah. I'm down for going in with knowledge, but I do think we'd be dumb if we didn't take advantage of the chunk of uninterrupted time we're given today and search his place."

Dorian pointed his index finger at us as a wicked grin twisted across his face. "See, that right there, that type of thinking is what got the two of you in trouble last time. You should've had a well-crafted plan. You damn sure shouldn't have gone into that place blind."

"I don't see what difference it would've made," I said. "We still managed to rescue Violet. We still got out of there in one piece."

"Yeah, but y'all had to kill someone to do it."

Coldness centered in my stomach. He was right. Maybe if we had thought things out and done a little recon, we would have been able to avoid killing Drew.

"I'm not saying we shouldn't do as you're suggesting," Eli insisted, speaking to Dorian. "All I'm saying is we might also want to take advantage of the situation. Get in and get out as quick as possible once we've made it through your checklist. There won't be a better time than this afternoon, especially if we aren't looking to have another fatality."

"You don't know that," Dorian insisted. "For all you know, a better time could present itself."

"Like when? And is that something you're wanting to risk?" I asked unable to keep my mouth shut. "When would you suggest we go inside? When he's home and at risk of hearing us sneaking around?"

"No, like when there's darkness to hide us. We need every advantage we can get. Darkness would help to hide us from any neighbors he may have."

"What if he doesn't have any?" I asked, unable to keep the anger from trickling into my words.

Dorian didn't back down either. Instead he narrowed his eyes. "What if he does?"

Eli stepped between us. "Enough. We don't have time for this. We'll do it Dorian's way. It might take a hell of a lot longer, and we might miss our only chance to grab Glenn if he's there, but it also might be safer in the long run," Eli said. He shifted his attention to me. "How's Violet doing? Did you check with your Gran to see if there's any update on her status?"

"No. I didn't check with her, but she bought stuff to make more concoctions today so I'm assuming things aren't going as she hoped," I said as I ran my fingers through my hair.

"Maybe you're a little too consumed with imprinting to be in the right mindset for the things that need to be done," Dorian spat.

I wanted to deck the guy. Who the hell did he think he was? This was definitely not the Dorian I witnessed with Sheila all the time. That Dorian seemed happy, kind, and slightly carefree. This guy...well, there was nothing to him besides darkness and hard, sharp edges. He was way too damn serious and an asshole. I opened my mouth to tell him so, but Eli spoke before I could.

"I said that's enough," Eli demanded.

Dorian released a long breath through gritted teeth. "Fine. Tell me everything you know about Violet's situation, Mina."

I pursed my lips. Was I going to be on trial again?

When Dorian glared at me, giving me a look that let me know he was growing impatient, I resisted the urge to flip him off and instead folded my arms across my chest.

"Two sides to every story, darlin'," he insisted.

I rolled my eyes. "I'm not sure where you want me to start. Do I need to start at the very second we found her, or would starting with when we realized there was an issue with her healing be sufficient enough?"

Yes, I was being a smart-ass, but he deserved it.

"Realizations and theories regarding her healing will work," Dorian insisted.

"Okay, well for starters, she hasn't healed. At all. There are still bruises and cuts all over her body that should have been healed days ago. Her ankle is still screwed up, and I'm not sure it will heal properly even with time."

"Why is she not healing? What are the theories surrounding that?" Dorian's brows pinched together. He'd lost his hard edge, and a little bit of his soft side was starting to shine through.

"We think she's been severed from her wolf," I said.

The look that crossed Dorian's face was one I could relate to. It was exactly how I felt when I first heard—completely submerged in unimaginable thoughts. No one ever wanted to think of what it would feel like to become severed from his wolf.

My thumb smoothed along the band of the silver moon ring Eli had given me.

"Does your Gran have any ideas as to how we might be able to get Violet's wolf back? Is it even possible?" Dorian asked.

"She's doing everything she can. This isn't something she's come across before." I tucked my hair behind my ears. "She's tried a few infusions of herbs and tinctures, but I don't think any of them have helped."

"Maybe that's something you should check out," Dorian insisted.

I nodded. "I will. At some point today."

Dorian paced while rubbing his jaw. "We have to fix this. She's too young to go through something like this. She didn't have time to enjoy her wolf."

I flinched at his words because that was what made it worse.

Violet hadn't been a wolf for a solid month yet. My teeth sank into my bottom lip as guilt crept in from the darkest corners of my mind.

I should've made sure she left the woods that night. I should have walked her to the edge that butted up against the trailer park. I should've done something more than what I had.

"We need a witch," Dorian said. "A witch might be able to help us tether her wolf back to her again."

"Is there a spell for that?" I asked.

"Witches have spells for everything," Eli insisted. Excitement hung in his voice, and I knew it was because he thought Dorian was on to something.

"What about a Caraway witch?" I asked. "Wouldn't one of them be willing to help?"

"For a price, maybe," Dorian said. "They are the most powerful, badass witches in town, though. If bringing back a severed wolf by magic can be done, there's no doubt in my mind they're powerful enough to do it."

"I know one," I admitted, thinking of Ridley. "I could probably talk to her and see if she'll ask her family to help."

"Okay, you focus on that while Eli and I scope out Peter's place," Dorian said.

"What? No. I'm coming with you."

Dorian shook his head. "There's no need. Eli and I can handle it. You go talk to the Caraway witch you know and find out if there's any way they can help Violet, if they know of a spell."

"I can call her later. I'm coming with you to Peter's."

If they happened to find Glenn while they were scoping out the place, I wanted to be there for it. No, I needed to be. His disappearance weighed too heavy on my heart.

"She's coming," Eli insisted. Either he was able to feel how much I wanted to be there, or he could see it written on my face. "Like she's said, she can call the Caraway witch she knows later. Right now, we don't need to waste any more time arguing. We need to get to Peter's and scope it out so we can make a game plan."

Dorian nodded. It was clear to see though from the look on his face that agreeing with Eli about me coming along was the last thing he wanted to do. "Fine, let's go."

11

The three of us loaded into Eli's navy blue truck. My skin tingled when he cranked the engine. Even though I knew Peter wouldn't be home, I still couldn't keep the anxiety prickling through my system at bay. It was safe to say a life of crime was not for me.

"What was the address again?" Eli asked.

Dorian rattled it off, but I barely heard him over the pounding of my heart. Maybe I should've stayed back and tried to get in touch with Ridley, while also checking up on Violet's status with Gran.

No. I was seeing this through like I'd said I would.

Eli turned out of the trailer park. It wouldn't take as long to get to Peter's place, but I wasn't sure how long it would take us to scope it out. Dorian seemed as though he was a play-by-the-rules kind of guy in situations like this, the type who didn't cut corners. I imagined he had a step by step program for how this was supposed to be done and would begin giving directions the second Peter's place came into view. I tried to think of that as a good thing while I stared out the windshield and willed my heart to return to its normal rhythm.

"That should be his driveway right there," Eli said. He pointed to a gravel road to my left twenty minutes later.

"The numbers match up," Dorian said as he glanced at a scrap of paper. "Why don't we head down the road a little farther and see if we can find a place to park that doesn't look suspicious. We can shift into our wolf forms and cut through the woods lining his driveway after."

"Sounds good to me," Eli said.

Peter also lived on a wooded lot similar to the one his brother had. Thank goodness. It meant there was minimal risk we would be seen. I thought to press the issue of there not being any neighbors and suggest again we use the time we were given to check the place out in-depth, but I decided against it. Dorian had made his position on that clear before we left.

A dirt area off the side of the road came into view. I wasn't sure if it was a turnaround or a place the property owner parked from time to time. It didn't matter. All that mattered was we had found a place to park.

The instant Eli cut his engine, the three of us climbed out of his truck and began shedding our clothes. Eli had Dorian stand at the tail end of the truck so he wouldn't be able to see me undressing. It was a sweet gesture, but one that wasn't necessary. Dorian had already seen me naked before. The entire pack had the night I became moon kissed.

Once I was undressed, I slipped off my silver jewelry,

ready to call my wolf forth. She was inside me, waiting anxiously to be set free. I felt the familiar heat envelop me as an image of her floated through my mind. Her big hazel eyes. Her soft, fluffy fur. Her tiny stature but fierce spirit.

She called to me, willing me to step aside.

Warm air filled with old wolf magic surrounded me. My lips twisted into a smile as I tipped my head up toward the sky, allowing the wind to caress my naked skin. My hair whipped around my face, and I closed my eyes while I waited for my wolf to take shape. When a chill zipped up my spine causing goose bumps to sprout across my bare skin, I knew the goddess of the moon was near. Her magic danced through the air around me, calling to my wolf. My wolf's howl ripped through the air when the three of us had completed the final phase of our transition into wolf form.

The familiarity of Eli and Dorian's wolf presence pulsed through me. Safety, comfort, and a sense of connectedness.

Eli stepped forward, his large wolf form getting into position to lead us toward Peter's. The three of us trekked through the woods alongside Peter's driveway. While it was nice to be hidden within thick foliage, I still preferred the coverage of darkness more. I searched for any sign of neighbors while we walked, but it seemed as though Peter enjoyed his solitude as much as Drew did.

We made it up a steep incline before the land finally leveled out again, revealing a large clearing with a house nestled in the middle.

Peter's house was beautiful. The place was like its own tiny paradise tucked into a thicket of woods.

The three of us stood still as we took in the area. I

assumed Dorian was already taking stock of things on his checklist. Eli was probably doing the same, but all I could do was soak in the beauty.

An acre or so of land had been cleared out, not entirely, but enough that there were only a few shade trees remaining. A pond that reminded me of the one Alec had taken me to caught my eye. I imagined it was probably overflowing with fish. The house was two stories and green. It had fun angles and a sharp pitch to its roof. The large wooden porch on the front had me thinking of cozying up with a blanket and mug of hot chocolate on a fall afternoon.

I loved this house. Everything about it.

My gaze drifted around as I tried to take note of some of the things Dorian had listed. There was no shed, but there was a detached carport a few feet away from the house. A riding lawnmower and shelves with various garden tools were underneath its cover.

There was no sign of Glenn.

Glenn.

At the thought of him, I began sniffing the air, trying to pick up his scent. Damp, wet earth. Pond water. No Glenn.

Eli nodded to Dorian, and then he started toward the house with a glance back at me. His eyes told me to follow. I did, hoping Dorian would pick up something related to Glenn and change his mind about not wanting to enter the house today.

When Dorian paused and nodded toward the roof of the porch, I thought maybe he had, but then I realized he wanted us to look at something. My gaze drifted to see what he was pointing out. A camera mounted to the porch roof. Dorian made a noise I could have sworn meant I told you so. If a wolf could grin, he definitely was. There was no doubt in my mind that once we were back in human form he'd tell me again how much of a good idea it was to scope places out before racing in blind.

The camera didn't bother me, though.

I knew we'd have to confront Peter at some point anyway. He had information we needed; information we couldn't get from anyone else now that Drew was dead.

I flashed Dorian a look I hoped he would interpret as *I don't give a crap* and started up the steps to the front porch. A low growl sounded from behind me, one I knew came from Dorian. He was warning me not to go near the door. I guess he thought I'd walk in even after everything he'd already said. I inched closer, testing his patience. He was really starting to piss me off. Eli let out a low growl that sent a shiver through me. He wanted me to get back too. I listened, but only because I had no intention of going inside alone anyway.

Eli rounded to the opposite side of the house when I crept down the stairs. I followed him, eager to put distance between myself and Dorian. Again, there didn't seem to be any sign of Glenn. Either he wasn't here, had never been here, or the last couple of rains had washed away his scent.

All were equally possible.

The only way we would know for sure if Glenn was here or had been was to step inside. Eli knew this. I knew he did. Still there was something holding him back, something allowing him to let Dorian make all the moves. Maybe it was guilt. Maybe he felt horrible for having killed Drew. If that was the case, I understood.

When we neared the back of the house, I noticed a window resting a few inches off the ground. It had to be a basement window. The house having a basement was good. It gave Peter a place to store things—like werewolves he'd helped abduct.

I pressed my face to the window and peered inside. At first, I could barely make anything out, but once my eyes adjusted to the dim light inside, I was able to make out shapes. A metal table. Shelving that ran floor to ceiling along the far wall. A chair in the center with thick straps dangling from it. A cage similar to the one Violet had been kept in.

My heart thundered at the sight of it. I tried to see if there were more beside it, but from the position of the window, I wasn't able to anything else against the wall. Glenn had to be here, though. This basement was the perfect place to keep him. We needed to get inside.

I howled and nodded to the window, begging Dorian and Eli to look. If this wasn't enough to get Dorian to change his mind about taking advantage of our current situation, I wasn't sure what would.

Time was on our side, and we would never be given another chunk like today unless another member of Peter's family died. Since I didn't see that happening in the near future, my gut was telling me it was now or never.

Eli and Dorian stepped to where I was and glanced inside the basement window. I imagined them turning around and giving me the go-ahead, so when that didn't happen, I grew angry. Instead Dorian took off for the woods, and Eli followed close behind him. Not able to comprehend what the hell they were doing, I opted to chase after them.

Once I reached the woods, I noticed Dorian already

shifting into his human form again. Good, it must mean he wanted to talk.

Even though my wolf was reluctant, I still managed to coax her to the side and let me have control again so I could shift back.

"Did you see that?" I asked as I struggled to catch my breath from having to force a change so fast. I pointed over my shoulder to the basement window, not caring I was naked while standing in the woods with two equally naked guys. All I could think about was how Glenn might be down there, waiting for us to find him. "Glenn could be in there. There's a cage. I couldn't see if there were more than one, but there could be. Glenn could be inside one right now."

"You don't know that," Dorian insisted.

"Those are similar to the cages we found Violet in," I insisted as though that proved it. I shifted my glance to Eli, begging him to back me up on this. He had to want to go in there as much as I did. "Tell him, Eli."

Eli ran a hand through his hair. "They are the same cages, but I couldn't see if Glenn was inside."

"Which is why we need to go inside to get a closer look," I said.

Dorian shook his head. "No. We can't. We have to stick to the plan."

"But we found what we were looking for," I insisted, waving my hands around wildly as anger and irritation toward Dorian and his stubbornness burned through my veins. "Maybe not who we were looking for, but he might actually be in there. We'll never know unless we step inside."

"There were files on the metal table I'd like to look at," Eli said, surprising me. He was all for heading inside, exactly as I was. We just needed to convince Dorian. "They might be able to tell us what Peter and his brothers have been doing, or what their boss wants with us. They could prove to be valuable."

Dorian leveled us with his gaze. "We are not stepping foot inside that house. We need to wait until nightfall and think this thing through. He had a camera posted on the porch, one on the side of the house, and one facing the driveway on the carport where the lawnmower is kept."

I wanted to shout at him. I wanted to beat him senseless. I wanted to scream. Instead I settled for lowering my voice, grinding my teeth together, and narrowing my eyes as I spoke. "None of that matters. Peter is going to see our faces anyway because I am not about to let him walk away from this unscratched. What he did, and what he's been a part of, isn't right."

"And what are you planning on doing, Miss Hothead?" Dorian asked in a sharp tone. "Bust inside with guns blazing? That's going to get you killed or hurt someone else. We have to be smart about this," he shouted as he tapped the side of his head with his index finger, insisting I use my brain.

"Then what do you suggest?" Eli asked. I could hear his irritation flaring through his words.

"I suggest we give it another day before we step inside. We come back tonight and see what this guy looks like, if he lets any animals out, if he lives alone. Then we go from there," Dorian said. I opened my mouth to tell him that wasn't happening, but he held up a hand asking me to give him another second to explain. "But, I know you won't go for that. Either one of you. So, I say we come back tonight at nightfall and break in. Now that I know there's a window we can fit through, we have no need to go in through one of the doors. We still need to be careful, though. There might be a security system attached to the house. An alarm to go with the cameras. Even though I know you don't care about being seen, an alarm would bring police here, which is something we don't need."

"Maybe police are exactly what we need. They'd see Glenn in there, beaten and locked in a cage. Then we could at least get Peter off the streets without having to take matters into our own hands," I insisted.

"No. Dealing with the police is the last thing we need," Eli said. "Dorian is right."

I hated to hear Eli agreeing with him. It made my blood boil.

"Fine, I guess we just head home, then, and wait until nightfall." Which seemed stupid to me, but apparently what I thought didn't matter.

"Shift back until we make it to the truck," Eli suggested.

I gave into my wolf again. It was easier this time because she was sitting there waiting.

By the time we made it back to the truck, I was so pissed off I could barely see straight. I couldn't believe we were leaving when we might be close to finding Glenn or at least to learning more about what we were dealing with. The files Eli had spotted would have been useful. Instead we were walking away empty-handed, thanks to Dorian.

After the three of us pulled our clothes back on, we piled into Eli's truck again and started for home. Silence built in the cab, but I was fine with it. There wasn't anything I had to say to either of them anyway. Instead I focused on what I'd say to Ridley when I asked for her help.

How would I even broach the topic?

When we made it to the trailer park, I'd decided on calling her and laying it all out there. She would probably appreciate that, since she didn't seem as though she was the type to beat around the bush. Also, it would be easier. And, at this point, I was all for easy.

12

Gran sat at the dining room table when I walked through the door. There was a pad of paper in front of her, and she was scrawling notes across its cream-colored pages. I imagined the notes were about what she'd tried on a Violet. Everything that had failed.

"Is there any improvement in her?" I asked, knowing Gran would know who I was speaking of without me mentioning her name.

I moved to the empty dining room chair beside her and sat. My gaze drifted over her perfect cursive handwriting etched across the notebook paper, but from the angle of the notebook and where I was sitting, I wasn't able to read anything she'd written.

"No. There's been no improvement," Gran said, and I swore I saw her deflate. Her shoulders slumped and her eyes grew weary as a nervous tremor I'd never heard before caused her words to waiver. "The swelling in her ankle has barely subsided, and her cuts and bruises still look the same.

Nothing I've given her seems to touch this. I can't will her wolf back. I decided all I can do is try to calm her enough so she might be able to connect with her wolf again on her own. I'm not sure it's going to work though," she said as she released a long exhale and smoothed a hand across her forehead.

"Do you think this is something the Caraway witches might be able to help us with?"

Gran's gaze lifted to lock with mine. "I'm not sure. I guess I haven't thought to ask."

"It might be a long shot, but maybe they have a spell to help bring Violet's wolf back."

"It's a good idea," Gran said as one of her wrinkled hands reached out to grab hold of mine. She squeezed and my heart overflowed with love for her. "The Caraway witches are strong. They come from a long line of old magic. If there were ever a line of witches to help in this situation, they would be it. The problem is, there's no telling what it will cost us to get their help. Magic always comes with a price."

I understood, but I didn't think the price they would ask would be any worse than what Violet was already going through. I imagined Violet would pay whatever cost they insisted upon to have her wolf back. Her family too. As her pack, we were part of that family. The cost to connect her to her wolf again was of no importance.

Gracie stepped into the room. Winston was clutched to her chest. So was his leash.

"I'm taking him for a walk," Gracie said as she eyed Gran and me. She knew we were talking about Violet. I could tell from the look on her face. "I'll be back in a little while."

Gran nodded as I stood to get a glass of water. Once

Gracie had stepped outside, I shifted my attention back to Gran.

"I think I should call Ridley," I said after taking a sip of water. "I'll ask her if there's anything her family can do to help."

I didn't give Gran a chance to answer before I started down the hall toward Gracie's and my shared bedroom. I scrolled through the contacts on my cell until I found Ridley's number. Sucking in a deep breath, I tapped on her name and put the phone to my ear.

"Hey," she answered on the third ring. "How are you?"

"I'm good," I said, surprised she knew who I was. We had exchanged numbers a while back but still had yet to text or call one another. "How are you?"

"I'm okay. A little shaken up, but okay. Shane brother's funeral was today. Benji asked me to go with him so I did. I've never been to a funeral before. It was pretty nerve-racking."

"I've never been to a traditional funeral before either, but I can imagine." I chewed my bottom lip, not sure when I should bring up what I needed from her.

Maybe this wasn't a good time.

"Alec seemed a little down. Obviously. I mean, his friend's brother just passed, but, um, are the two of you okay?"

Dread pooled in the pit of my stomach. The last thing I figured we'd talk about was Alec. "I think we will be. One day. Right now, Alec just needs time."

"You broke up with him." There wasn't judgment in her tone or anger. In fact, it wasn't even a question but more of a statement.

"I did. It was the right thing to do."

"I figured it would happen eventually. The two of you aren't compatible. You have another side I don't think he would be able to handle. Not in the long run, at least. Even if the two of you stayed together, Alec would never fit in with your pack. It's just the way things are."

She knew what I was. I guess I'd always known she did.

"Yeah, I know. It just sucks it took me so long to see it. I feel like I led him on."

"You did," Ridley said without hesitation. I shifted around on my feet, waiting for her to berate me and this conversation to head south. "I can understand why, though. We all want to be normal, Mina. Alec represented normalcy to you. That's understandable."

I was glad I'd called her. In fact, I wasn't sure why I hadn't called her before now, even if it was just to talk. Ridley understood what I was going through, because she was part of the supernatural world too.

"Okay, enough of that," she muttered. "What did you call me for? I doubt it was to talk about breaking up with Alec."

Straight to the point. I liked this girl.

"I need a favor. Actually, I'm not even sure if you'll be able to help, but I'm hopeful. I need to know if you have access to a particular kind of spell, something that might help a pack member who has been severed from her wolf find her way back."

Silence passed through the phone. I pulled it away from my ear and glanced at the screen, thinking our connection had been dropped, but it hadn't. The timer still ticked away, counting how long we'd been on the phone together.

"Oh, wow. That sounds pretty serious," Ridley finally said.

"It is."

"I'm sure my aunt would know of a spell that might help, but I don't know what the cost would be."

"As in how much money? That's not the issue. I'm sure the pack can come up with whatever it is." I hoped, anyway. None of us were rich. I mean, we did live in a trailer park. However, I was positive if we combined all of our resources we'd be able to come up with enough money to get Violet what she needed.

"No. I'm not talking about money. When it comes to magic, there's always a cost, and nine times out of ten it has nothing to do with money."

Unease pickled across my skin. I moved to sit on my bed and situated my back against the wall. "Oh. Okay, gotcha."

"Can you tell me a little about the situation? Any details would help my aunt figure out the direction she needs to go with the spell, but it would also help me. There is a chance I might not have to go to her. I might be able to find something on my own that would help."

"The girl is sixteen. She was abducted by someone and left for a couple days in a cage without access to silver," I said, trying to be careful not to mention Drew's name. I didn't want to tell her any information that might cause my pack or myself any harm. The less she knew about that aspect, the better. "Do you know what the connection is between us and silver?" I didn't know how much I needed to explain to her when it came to werewolves.

"I do. I studied up on the two most known creatures here before I moved. Your pack and the Montevallo family of vampires," Ridley admitted. She was smart. I didn't think that would've been something I would have thought to do. "How do you know her wolf has been severed? What are the signs and symptoms?"

"She's not healing. She has a few bruises and cuts from when she was abducted that should've healed days ago but haven't. They are fading but at a normal human rate. Same with her broken ankle. It should have already healed by now but hasn't. When she was found, she was completely naked and devoid of her silver jewelry."

Papers moving on her end of the phone caught my attention. Was she taking notes?

"Okay, I'll look into it and see what I can find. I'll get back to you tomorrow."

"Thanks," I said. "I'll let the others now I've got a kickass Caraway witch on it."

"I don't know about being kickass, but you can definitely say you have a Caraway witch on it," Ridley insisted with a chuckle. "Talk to you soon."

"Okay, thanks again," I said before I hung up.

I left my room and started down the hall, passing Gracie and Winston along the way. She was talking to him like he was a baby and scratching behind his ears. The sight of the two of them had my lips curling into a small grin.

"Hey, where's Gran?" I called back to her as I noticed Gran was no longer at the table.

"In the garden," Gracie said.

I headed outside, eager to tell Gran that Ridley had agreed to help. She was where Gracie said she'd be. With her pruning shears in hand and a wicker basket at her side, Gran made her way around her small garden gathering clips of herbs.

"Need any help?" I asked as I stepped inside the fenced in area.

Gran shifted to face me. A skeptical gleam entered her eyes. I knew it was because it was rare I ever offered to help with anything garden related. "Why? Is there something you need to talk to me about, or do you need money?"

I always needed money, but that wasn't what this was about. "I just got off the phone with Ridley Caraway. She's going to help us find a way to bring Violet's wolf back."

"How?" Gran plucked a couple sprigs off a rosemary plant.

"She took some notes from me, and she said she's going to see what she can find out for us. If she can't find anything, she'll involve her aunt," I said as I glanced at the plant nearest me. Its leaves looked withered. "Have you watered your garden recently?"

Gran glanced at me. "Asks the girl who knows nothing about gardening."

My cheeks heated. "Sorry. The plants just look like they could use some water. Their leaves seem wilted."

"I watered them yesterday. We're supposed to get rain over the next couple of days, and I didn't want to water them too much, so they probably are thirsty." Gran placed a hand on her hip, making it clear she didn't like me criticizing her skills when it came to taking care of her own garden. "Continue with what Ridley plans to do."

"That's it," I said with a shrug. "She said she's going to look into it. If she can't find anything out on her own, she'll ask her aunt. She did say she'd have something to me by tomorrow, and it would probably come with a cost."

"Of course, all magic does. I've told you this before." She

walked to the other side of her garden. "I wonder what it will be this time."

"This time?" When was the last time we had asked the Caraway witches for help with anything?

"Of course," Gran insisted. "The full moon ceremonies are hidden by their magic."

"Right. I forgot about that." The cost of that had been for us to keep vampires out of Mirror Lake with the exception of the Montevallo family. It was a steep price, one that cost us a lot of time and manpower. I was sure whatever they asked for next would be the same.

"The only way they'll help us is if there's something else they desire we can get them," Gran said as she bent to focus on a basil plant. It looked as though something had chewed up its leaves.

I wondered what the Caraway witches would want from us this time. It didn't seem as though there was much we could give.

Either way, Violet getting her wolf back would be worth it. I hoped whatever they did—whatever spell or potion they created—it could be easily duplicated because I had a feeling whenever we found Glenn we would need a second dose.

13

It was just starting to get dark when I made it to Eli's place. Dorian was already there. He insisted we go over everything from our first trip to Peter's again as well as anything I learned from Ridley. Also, he told us the plan he had crafted for the night and stressed numerous times how much he wanted us to stick to it.

"We know our point of entry is the basement window. It's large enough for all of us to crawl through. This makes the whole situation one hundred times safer because we don't have to travel through the house trying to find our way to the basement. It's a straight shot. Which means there's minimal risk you guys will screw up this situation," Dorian said as he paced back and forth in Eli's kitchen.

"We didn't screw up the last time. We rescued Violet, or have you forgotten?" I snapped, hating the way he talked down to us. He was supposed to be our chaperone, yes, but nowhere in the description did it say he needed to be an asshole.

"A human was killed. I'd say that's a pretty big screw-up." Dorian's eyes narrowed.

"Moving forward," Eli said. He seemed as annoyed as I was Dorian kept bringing that night up.

"Right. One by one, we will enter the basement window. There didn't seem to be any pets, but that's something I'll have to check tonight before we make a move."

"What do you plan on doing if he does have a pet?" I asked with more attitude than was necessary. Apparently there was no better feeling than grilling Dorian.

He flashed me a wicked grin. "If it's a cat, nothing. I doubt a cat would do anything to alert him we were there. If it's a dog, I have a special treat for it." He reached into the front pocket of his dark jeans and pulled out a Ziploc bag with two dog treats inside.

"What's so special about them?" Eli asked.

"I purchased some dog tranquilizers and slipped one into each. If he does have any dogs, they won't be a problem for long. They'll be sleeping like a baby in seconds."

Well, at least he wasn't going to hurt them. I hated to admit it, but Dorian's idea was pretty good.

"I know we're there to search for Glenn," Eli said. "But, like I said before, I'd like to get my hands on the files I saw. I think we would be able to learn a lot from them."

"The files are a top priority," Dorian insisted. "We have to find out the inner workings of this situation."

"Sounds good," I said as I clapped my hands together. "Let's get this show on the road."

I didn't want to hang around much longer. I was beginning to get antsy. I needed to know if Glenn was there. If he was, I was going to be so pissed at Dorian. I thought of what

I'd say to him as the three of us piled into Eli's truck and headed to Peter's place.

We parked in the same space as before. This late at night, there seemed to be even less traffic than before, which was a good thing.

"Let's shift and head to Peter's the way we did earlier—by sticking to the woods that line the driveway. Be on alert this time, Peter could be home, and there's a chance he might not be alone," Dorian insisted as he walked to the end of the truck to take off his clothes again.

My heart dropped to my toes at the mention of Peter possibly not being alone. After the day he had, there was a good chance someone would be at his house, consoling him. It was another reason why we should've done this earlier. Screw Dorian and his well-thought-out plan. Sometimes going into things blind was the best way to handle them.

I pulled off my clothes and tossed them onto the seat of the truck. My gaze drifted to Eli. His muscles were tense, and his jaw was hard set. I didn't think he liked having Dorian give him orders.

Once the three of us shifted, we started up the driveway by keeping to the woods like we had last time. Dorian had the bag of dog treats in his mouth. It crinkled with every step he took, causing him to make more noise than Eli and me. When Peter's house came into view, I relaxed at the sight of only one vehicle in the driveway. Lights were on inside but only on the main floor. The upstairs was dark. This made me think he was still awake.

Dorian dropped the treat bag and sniffed the air. I knew he was searching for the scent of any pets Peter might have let out when he got home. I sniffed the air too, but didn't pick up anything.

We were off to a smooth start it seemed. I was grateful.

The three of us rounded the house until we came to the basement window. Dim lighting cast through the space, but it wasn't enough for me to think Peter was inside. It looked as though one of the machines had been turned on and was casting a glow through the room.

Eli pushed on the window with his snout. It popped open with ease. I held my breath as Eli leaped into the basement. Dorian went next. I hung around outside, staring in the window and listening. Eli's green eyes locked with mine. They seemed to beckon me. I finally gave in and leaped through the window after them. Once I was inside, I headed for the cages. There were three, exactly like in Drew's basement. Each of them seemed made of the same material. There was still a bucket in the corner, but instead of a blanket on the cold concrete floor, there were cots.

Glenn was lying on one.

He didn't look as banged up as what Violet had when we first found her, but he still had seen better days. Bruises lined his inner elbows. Were they track marks? I was sure they weren't self-inflicted, but he did look like a junkie. Peter must have been doing some heavy testing on him or keeping him drugged.

I couldn't believe he'd been here the entire time. My insides burned with anger. Before I realized I was doing it, I'd pushed my wolf to the side and shifted back into human form.

"He's been here the whole time," I said in a hushed

whisper as I took in the sight of Glenn. "We could have easily gotten him out earlier."

A familiar charge zipped through the air as Eli shifted back as well.

"Glenn. Hey, buddy," Eli said as he rushed to his cage. "We're here for you."

There was no response from him. I wondered if he'd been drugged with the same stuff Violet had when we'd rescued her. If so, it was going to make it ten times harder to get him out of here quietly. At least Dorian was here to help Eli carry his dead weight, because I wasn't sure I would be much help getting him through the basement window.

Speaking of Dorian, where was he?

I glanced around, searching for him. He'd leapt through the window before me so I knew he was here somewhere. I spotted him near the basement window, gazing out as though he was making sure the coast was clear. I wasn't sure when he'd done it, but at some point between entering the basement and now, Dorian had shifted back into his human form as well.

"We might want to get out of here in a minute," Dorian said as though he could feel my heated gaze on him.

"Wasn't that the plan all along?" I snapped. "Get in and get out as quickly as possible?"

I couldn't stand to breathe the same air as him right now, let alone speak to him.

"Yeah, well." Dorian shifted around to face me. The worried gleam in his eyes sent alarm nipping at my insides. "We've got company."

"What do you mean?" Eli asked. He abandoned Glenn and headed for the basement window.

Headlights shifted through the room. Both Dorian and Eli jumped out of the way before the light could reach them. I remained still, frozen.

Someone was here. This was so not good.

"Two people. Both men. I'd say about six-foot-tall each," Dorian whispered as he glanced out the window, carefully assessing the new people who had arrived. "Shit."

"What?" I asked in a hushed whisper.

"Both of them are vampires," Dorian answered.

Vampires? What the hell were vampires doing at Peter's house?

"They don't look like they're from the Montevallo family either," Eli added. "I've never seen these guys before."

My heart raced inside my chest. The only thing I could think about was getting Glenn out of here. I jerked at the bars of his cage door, praying it wouldn't be locked. The thing didn't budge. I glanced around the metal shelving unit closest to me, searching for something I might be able to use to pick the lock with quickly. We had to get Glenn out of here. He had to come with us. There was no way I was going to leave him again.

"Help me find something to pick this lock with," I insisted. Didn't they understand we needed to move, we needed to act? We were here to rescue Glenn, not stare at vampires all night.

"No," Dorian said. "As soon as they step into the house, we need to get the hell out of here."

"What?" I snapped. I glanced over my shoulder at him. He couldn't be serious. Glenn was right here. We needed to get him out. Who knew if we would have another chance? "No. We have to rescue him."

Eli jumped into action and searched through the drawers to one of the stainless-steel tables. When he found something that looked sharp, he stepped to my side. "Watch out. Let me see if I can get it unlocked with this."

I stepped out of Eli's way, grateful he was at least on my side. He fiddled with the lock but didn't seem to be having any luck.

"It's too thick. I need something thinner," Eli insisted as he threw what he'd been holding down and begin searching frantically for something else.

"We don't have time for this," Dorian insisted from where he stood at the window. "They just went inside. And from the looks on their faces, I'd say they aren't happy to be here."

"I'm not happy to be here either," I snapped as I continued searching for anything that might help open the lock.

Loud footsteps sounded above us. All the breath left the room as the three of us froze, listening to where they were headed. My eyes zeroed in on the basement door at the top of the stairs. The sound of a key being shoved into the door floated through the air. A light flicked on, illuminating the stairs seconds before the door opened.

"We have to get out of here now," Dorian whispered. The intensity behind his words sent goose bumps pickling across my skin. He was right. We need to get out now or else we risked being caught, but what about Glenn?

"Mina, come on," Eli insisted. His fingers gripped my wrist and pulled me away from Glenn's cage toward the open basement window.

Dorian had already slipped outside. He reached through the window for me. Between him and Eli, I barely had to climb out the basement myself. They hoisted me up and pulled me out with little effort on my part.

Footfalls echoed through the basement as more than one person descended the stairs.

"A little birdie told us your brother is no more," a rough voice said.

"That's right," Peter answered. The tremor in his voice was audible. Either he hadn't been expecting them, or he was scared shitless they were here. Maybe it was both.

"Why do you think that is?" the man with the deep, rough voice asked.

"It was an accident. He was drunk and fell down the stairs."

"Come now," the other vampire said. "You don't believe that. Do you?"

Dorian reached out to help Eli out of the basement, but he didn't accept it. Instead his gaze snapped to lock with mine. Something shifted through his eyes, but I wasn't able to decipher what it was before he dashed away from the window.

What the hell was he doing? He needed to get out of there.

My gaze drifted to the stairs. A pair of dress shoes and black slacks caught my attention. Eli was almost out of time.

I opened my mouth to say something, but Dorian's hand clamped over it. His hot breath warmed my ear as he shushed me quietly. My heart stalled out as I shifted my gaze back to Eli. He'd doubled back for the files stacked on one of the stainless-steel counters. When he passed them through the window, I grabbed them at the same time Dorian gripped

Eli's arms. In seconds, Eli was at my side and the window was closed securely behind him.

Eli's arms wrapped around me as he pulled me away from the window. I struggled to catch my breath while my fingers dug into his forearm and crushed the files to my chest. I wanted to shout at him. I wanted to slap him silly for having scared me. I did none of those things because even though the basement window was closed, I could still hear movement from inside. This meant any noise I made they would be able to hear. Vampires had just as good of hearing as we did.

"Did your brother piss someone off?" I heard one of the vampires ask.

I wiggled out of Eli's grip and peeked through the window inside the basement.

"I don't think so," Peter said as he moved around the room, clicking on the lights.

Surprisingly, the vampires didn't seem bothered by the bright florescent lights. I didn't know much about vampires, but I had always thought they had a sensitivity to light.

"Drew wasn't much of a people person. There's a good chance quite a few people in town were pissed at him. But, like I said, his death was ruled an accident. He was drunk and fell down the stairs to his basement." Peter's voice still wavered when he spoke. It caused him to fumble on a couple of words.

"Really?" the vampire with the deep, rough voice asked. He had a wide scar that ran along the small section of skin between the base of his nose and his upper lip, disfiguring it. "Because the same little birdie we spoke to earlier said Drew was trying to double-cross Regina."

My grip on the files tightened as I continued to stare into the window. Who was Regina?

"Drew wasn't trying to double-cross anyone," Peter insisted.

"Are you saying he didn't have any plans to snag another werewolf? One that happened to be female for someone else?" the vampire with the scar asked as he reached inside the drawer on the stainless-steel counter Eli had left open.

"Not that I know of." There was hesitation in Peter's voice. Obviously, he wasn't one hundred percent sure Drew wouldn't do such a thing. He also knew if Drew had attempted such a feat, he was going to be in trouble for it.

Would Peter pay the consequences for his brother's actions?

"You're saying you had absolutely no idea your brother was working with someone else?" the vampire pressed farther. A wild look flared in his dark eyes, as if he enjoyed seeing Peter on edge and having the upper hand.

My stomach rolled because he looked like the type of guy who got off on inflicting pain on others.

"No," Peter said with a firm voice. Through the distance, I could see his eye twitch. He was lying.

The vampire with the scar who seemed to be running the show must have noticed as well, because he chuckled. I watched as he took a step back and handed the other vampire a scalpel.

"You had better be glad your brother is already dead, and it happened to be a quick death," the other vampire said as he pressed the tip of the sharp scalpel to his index finger, slicing it open. Drops of dark blood dripped onto the stainless-steel counter in front of him. "Because if we had taken him in and passed him over to Regina, she would've tortured the poor soul until he begged for death for his betrayal."

Peter swallowed hard, but he didn't speak. He did, however, take a step back, placing more space between him and the vampires.

"Now, I'm only going to ask you this once," the vampire holding the scalpel said. "Who was your brother working with?"

"He wasn't working with anyone," Peter insisted.

The vampire with the scar across his upper lip laughed, drawing my attention back to him. "Benny, let him know how wrong of an answer that was."

It happened in seconds. The vampire with the scalpel, Benny, lunged toward Peter. He stabbed him in the hand. The scalpel went so deep it pinned his hand to the stainless-steel counter. Peter screamed. It echoed through the basement, sending a shiver along my spine.

"You should've told the truth," Benny said. "Now, you know there are consequences for lying."

Peter grabbed the scalpel and pulled it from his hand. Blood splattered across the counter as another scream propelled past his clamped lips. The sight of the blood pooling across the counter had me looking to both of the vampires. A sick sense of excitement twisted the vampire with the scars features.

Who the hell was this guy?

"Let's try this again," the vampire with the scar said as he stepped forward and took another scalpel from in the drawer. I was beginning to feel as though he was the boss of the other. Maybe even this Regina chick's right-hand man. "We know your brother was working with someone and we need a name.

Regina does not like to be double-crossed, in case you haven't figured that out by now."

"I can't," Peter whimpered as he cradled his hand to his chest and shook his head back and forth.

Oh shit, these guys were going to kill him if he didn't say who Drew had been working with.

"Wrong answer," the vampire with the scar said before his arm lifted with the scalpel. His wrist flicked, and the thing flew through the air like a throwing knife until it landed in Peter's shoulder.

Peter cried out. My stomach somersaulted, but I still continued to stare. I needed to pay attention. It was the only way I was going to find out who Regina was. And Glenn, I needed to make sure he was going to be okay. These guys seemed hell-bent on finding out who Drew had been working with. I prayed they weren't also here to get Glenn.

"I'm starting to lose my patience," the vampire with the scar muttered as he rummaged through the other drawers of the table. Apparently, scalpels weren't doing the trick anymore. "You need to tell me who your brother was working for and you need to tell me now. Regina does not value your life anymore. If that's what you're thinking, you're wrong. She doesn't take kindly to those who double-cross her. Nor does she like their family. Wouldn't it be a pity if your poor mother had to bury two more sons days after she buried the first?"

"Already have a couple of guys scoping out that younger brother of yours." The other vampire smirked. "Looks like he'd be easy prey."

Shane. They were talking about Shane.

While I didn't like him, it didn't mean I wanted him to

die at the hands of some pissed off vampires. Nobody deserved to go out that way.

"Leave my brother alone," Peter begged. He backed himself up against a wall and closed his eyes. "Please."

"Tell me what I want to know, and maybe I'll consider it," the vampire with the scar said as he swirled around a pair of pliers in his hand. I didn't want to think of what he planned to do to Peter with them.

"It's a friend of our family. Drew was working with a family friend," Peter said.

"Vague answer. I don't like vague answers," the vampire with the scar snarled.

"Better give him a name," Benny insisted.

Peter opened his eyes, but he didn't speak. Not until the vampire with the scar took a step toward him.

"David," Peter shouted. "David Thomas."

I knew that name. It was Alec's uncle.

That must be why Eli's dad had seen him talking with vampires. He was planning to double-cross Regina.

"See, that wasn't so hard. Now that I have a name, I'll be taking what we came for," the vampire with the scar said as he set the pliers down on the counter. I watched as he made his way to Glenn's cage.

No!

They were going to take him. This was it. The moment where we lost Glenn for good.

Eli grabbed my arm, and I knew he was trying to hold me at bay. I couldn't look at him. I couldn't look at Dorian. All I could do was watch as Glenn slipped away.

"Open it," the vampire with the scar insisted.

Peter made his way to the cage. He pulled out a set of keys from his pocket, and with shaky hands opened the door.

Anger thrashed through my insides. Glenn was going to be taken by these goons right in front of me. A small gasp escaped me when the vampire with the scar over his lip nodded for Benny to retrieve Glenn. He stepped inside the cage and jerked Glenn to his feet. Eli's grip on me tightened. My wolf howled inside my head, detesting the sight of a pack member being taken to who knew where by vampires. I clamped my mouth shut and squeezed the files tighter against my chest. Surely Dorian and Eli weren't going to sit here and continue to watch this. Surely Eli was telling me to be quiet and remain calm because he had a plan to stop them, and it involved the element of surprise.

"Oh, and Peter," the vampire with the scar said as Benny started toward the stairs with Glenn. "We want what Drew got for the other guy."

Peter shook his head wildly. "He didn't get anything for them."

"We know he did."

"I don't know anything about that order. I wasn't a part of it," Peter insisted.

"Do you think I give a shit?" the vampire with the scar asked. He reached in the open drawer beside him and grabbed out another scalpel. Mischief flashed through his dark eyes as he stalked toward Peter. "Word is, he had his hands on a female wolf. We want one too. Now that your brother is dead, the task falls to you."

"But that's not something I do. I'm not a hunter," Peter blubbered.

"Again, do you think I give a shit?" the vampire asked. He

pressed the scalpel into Peter's neck. A thin line of blood trickled down from the wound. The vampire flicked his tongue out and licked the area clean. "Like I said, now that he's gone, the task falls to you. Regina wants a female wolf. And she's giving you one week to obtain one, which is fairly generous, considering."

"Fine, fine!" Peter shouted as he held up his hands. His head was angled to the side, exposing his neck, and his eyes were squeezed shut. His body trembled with fear. The guy was petrified. I guess I didn't blame him. After all, he was only human.

A commotion came from the front of the house. Eli released in his grip on me and tapped my knee to get my attention. When I glanced at him, he nodded toward the woods and motioned for me to follow. Dorian was already halfway there. I hadn't realized he'd left my side. The three of us barely made it to the thicket of the woods before Benny rushed down the porch steps with Glenn.

I held my breath as I waited for Eli and Dorian to do something in order to stop Glenn from being taken.

They did nothing except watch, which was exactly what I did.

"Aren't you going to do something?" I whispered to Eli.

He placed a finger to his lips as his eyes locked with mine and shook his head. My entire body deflated.

"We have to do something. We can't just let Glenn be taken," I insisted as my stomach rolled and my heart thundered against my rib cage. "There are three of us and two of them."

"Keep your voice down," Dorian scolded. "I know this looks bad, but the main guy running this is older than he looks, which means he's stronger than you're giving him credit for. If we attack, not only is there a risk we might not make it out alive, but there's also a chance Glenn might not either."

"So, what are we supposed to do, then? Hide in the woods and watch?" I asked.

Neither Dorian nor Eli spoke. I guess that was answer enough.

My gaze drifted back to Benny. I watched as he lugged Glenn toward a dark vehicle in the driveway. He shoved him in the backseat and then climbed behind the steering wheel. My heart stopped when I heard the engine start. The vampire with the scar came out of the house and situated himself in the passenger seat. All the breath left my lungs as I watched the vehicle turn around and disappear down Peter's driveway.

The vampires were gone, and so was Glenn.

14

I stood frozen, while staring into the space the vampires' vehicle had previously occupied. Glenn had been in our sight, and we'd let him be taken.

"He's gone. We let them take him." My voice shook as I spoke.

"It was the only thing we could do," Dorian insisted.

"No. It wasn't." I shook my head. My gaze shifted between Eli and Dorian as disappointment built within me. "We could have done so much more than stand here in the shadows. We could've fought. We could've gotten Glenn out of here earlier when Peter was occupied and the coast was clear. There was a hell of a lot more we could've done, but we didn't do anything," I said through gritted teeth.

Rage burned through me, but it was nothing compared to the guilt I felt. Three times I could have helped Glenn but didn't. Instead I'd done nothing. What kind of a pack member did that make me? Not a good one, that was for damn sure.

Unless...

"Peter is supposed to get a female wolf for them like Drew did," I said, staring at the front of the house. "I'm going to be that wolf."

"What?" Eli snapped. "That's insane. No, you're not."

I shifted to glance at him and looked in his eyes. "I am. It's the right thing to do." My words cracked with emotion, but I kept going. "I just stood by and watched Glenn be taken. It's the third time I could've done something to help him, and I didn't."

"It wasn't your responsibility," Dorian insisted. "You weren't even supposed to be here tonight. You were supposed to be handling the Caraway witches, helping them find something that might help Violet."

I ignored Dorian. My focus was on Eli. Convincing him this was the right thing to do wasn't going to be easy. There was no way he would let me walk into danger without putting up a fight.

"It's the only way. Peter is supposed to get a female werewolf. Who else would you rather him take?" I held Eli's gaze, waiting for him to name someone else, anyone besides me.

Eli worked his jaw back and forth as he held my gaze. "No one. No one else gets taken. Enough damage has already been done to our pack. I'll be damned if I let another pack member be handed over, especially you," Eli insisted.

I squeezed the files I'd been holding tighter against my chest and let out a long sigh. "That's not going to work. The only way we're going to find Glenn now is if we have someone on the inside. Someone like me."

He had to see how right I was. He had to see how this was the only way.

"I hate to say it, but she might be right," Dorian surprised me by saying. I shifted to look at him, searching to see if he was serious. He seemed to be. "There's more at stake here than rescuing Glenn, though. We need to figure out who Regina is and what it is she wants with us."

"Right," I agreed. "And we need to figure out where she's running this operation from."

Eli shook his head. If looks could kill, both Dorian and I would be dead.

"I don't like it. It's too risky," he said.

I reached for his hand and intertwined my fingers through his. "Maybe, but it's a risk I'm willing to take if it helps our pack. If it helps bring Glenn home where he belongs. If it puts an end to all of this."

"I'm not willing to let you take this risk, though." His voice was raw and emotional. It cracked when he spoke.

"I don't think she's going to give you a say in the matter," Dorian insisted, and for a second time in the span of a few minutes, I agreed with him.

"He's right. I'm not." I lifted to the tips of my toes and placed a kiss on Eli's cheek. "Let's head inside and talk to Peter. There's still information we can get out of him, and it would probably be best if we let him know what we're doing before anyone else in the pack gets hurt."

Dorian chuckled. "I didn't think I would ever say this, but I agree with everything you said."

"You better because there isn't a chance in hell you'd be able to talk me out of this now." My gaze drifted to Eli as I turned to face him. "Sorry, but neither can you."

A frown pulled at the corners of his lips. "I know." Eli

squeezed my hand in his, but he didn't look at me. Part of me thought maybe he couldn't. "Let's talk to Peter."

Finally, something was going the way I wanted it to. I was calling the shots, and they were good enough shots for the guys to listen. It felt good.

We started toward the house.

"We should head back through the basement window," I said. "It will save us time and give us an element of surprise."

I made it to the window first. The lights were still on. I could see Peter sitting on the floor, assessing each area he was bleeding from with his good hand. I placed the files I'd been holding on the ground beside me and knocked on the window. Peter flinched. Fear shifted across his face, but it disappeared when his gaze landed on me. I wasn't sure if it was because I didn't seem threatening enough or if it was because I was naked. Either way, it was safe to say he had no idea how much of a threat I could be.

When Peter stood, I pushed the window open and a slipped inside. He didn't say a word to stop me. Was he in shock?

Eli and Dorian entered the basement behind me, but still Peter displayed no reaction.

"I know who you are," Peter said. His voice sounded flat and weighed down by exhaustion. "I know who you're looking for, too. He's no longer here." He held up his good hand in an effort to keep us where we were.

I imagined his mind going crazy with thoughts of how scary his night had already been. Was it hard for him to process that once the vampires left, a group of werewolves came in search of their stolen pack member? I bet he was thinking how bad his luck was.

"We know. We saw everything." I took a tentative step forward. "We've come to offer you a deal."

"A deal? What kind of deal?" He seemed flabbergasted we would even suggest such a thing, considering.

I paused in my forward motion once I reached the stainless-steel counter separating us. His blood still coated a small section of the counter, serving as a reminder of how horrible his night had been.

The tiniest ping of sympathy shifted through me. It was short-lived.

"I want to know everything you know," I said as I leaned against the counter, hoping I looked more intimidating than I felt. "Who is Regina? What does she want with the members of my pack? Where she's keeping them? I want to know it all."

Peter swallowed hard. "I'm afraid I can't give you that information."

"Is that so?" Dorian insisted from somewhere behind me. I didn't glance at him to see the expression on his face. I didn't have to, because I could tell from the way Peter's face paled, Dorian looked intimidating as hell.

"If I tell you, she'll kill me," Peter insisted.

"And what do you think we will do to you if you don't give us the information we're asking for?" Eli asked.

I couldn't deny the sense of excitement slithering through me from playing the role of a bad guy in order to scare the shit out of someone who was so deserving.

Peter didn't say another word until Eli and Dorian took a step forward.

"Okay, okay!" he shouted as he held both hands up in front of him. "I'm probably going to die anyway. There's not a chance in hell I'm going to be able to get them what they want."

"Actually, in exchange for information, I'm willing to offer myself up as your female werewolf," I somehow said without a hint of a waiver entering my voice.

Peter blinked. At first, I thought I saw a tentative smile build at the corner of his lips, but it dissolved as his eyes narrowed.

Did he not believe me?

"I don't know much," Peter insisted as he gripped his hurt hand to his chest.

"But you know something, which is more than we do. That's enough," I insisted.

Peter's chin dipped into his chest as he exhaled a long breath. "Okay. Where do I even start?"

"Do you know who Regina is?" Eli asked. It was as good a place as any.

"She's a vampire who lives in the city," Peter said. "I've never met her. I've only met with her guys."

"How did you first start working with her?" I asked, wondering how a seemingly weak guy like him managed to get caught up in a mess like this.

"Drew, my brother, came to me with an offer. He said there was a chance for us to make money while we rid our town of dangerous creatures such as yourselves," Peter insisted without meeting any of our gazes. "It wasn't the option of money that grabbed my attention, though; it was being able to study you. That's what I cared about most."

"Why?" I didn't understand what was so fascinating about us.

"Your healing capabilities are impressive. So is your

speed and the fact you can shift into an animal. I wanted to figure out how it all worked. The scientific side of everything called me."

"Did you learn anything?" Dorian asked.

Peter shook his head. "No. It's all still a mystery. I'm guessing it's something in your blood, but it could take years of research before I even come close to figuring anything out."

"Is that what you've been doing here? Studying? Testing for your own personal knowledge?" I asked, thinking there had to be more to it than that.

"Yes and no. I was studying your kind for my own knowledge, but my job in this whole scheme was to test you. Make sure those captured were strong and their blood was pure." His gaze lifted to lock with mine.

"Strong enough for what?" I asked, feeling sick to my stomach.

The ghost of a smile touched Peter's lips. The sight of it had me fearful of what his next words might be. "To have your blood harvested. We've learned over time the weak ones either don't produce well, or they don't survive the process."

Dizziness slipped through me.

How many of our pack members had they abducted? How far back did this scheme of theirs go?

"What good is werewolf blood to a vampire? We aren't on their menu," Dorian said.

Peter chuckled. It was a wicked chuckle that had my skin crawling. "Or are you?"

"What are you talking about?" Eli asked. "Vampires feed off humans. Some feed off animals, but it's rare. Humans are their weakness. Everyone knows it."

"Correct, if we're discussing a vampire's diet, but we are

not," Peter insisted. The smirk on his face grew and it took everything in my power to not slap it off his face.

"What are we talking about then?" Dorian asked before I could.

"A vampire's ability to get high and their current drug of choice in the city."

The concrete floor beneath my feet felt as though it suddenly fell away. I had no idea what Peter was talking about, but I knew it wasn't good.

"It seems as though this is all new knowledge to you," Peter said. "Maybe I had more information to pass along than I thought."

"If you're done gloating," Eli snarled. "Tell us more about this drug floating through the city and what it has to do with us."

Peter straightened his back as the smirk fell away from his face. It was clear he didn't want to piss us off any more than he already had, especially not Eli or Dorian. I still didn't think he viewed me as a threat. "Right. Well, when your blood is mixed with common ginseng, it creates a drug that seems to be irresistible to vampires. In fact, it's selling like hot cakes in the city. They call it Abstraction. It's supposed to make them feel completely eutrophic, the way humans do when they're on Ecstasy."

Great. Our blood was being harvested from us so vampires could feel good.

"How long has this been going on?" Dorian asked.

"Years," Peter answered without hesitation.

Years? How was it possible something like this had been happening right under our nose? How could we have been blind for so long?

"You're wrong if you think you can stop it," Peter said, breaking through my thoughts. "Even if you kill me—like you killed my brother—Regina won't stop. She might not take more wolves from your pack, but it doesn't mean she won't find others."

"Okay. This is what's going to happen," Eli insisted. "Dorian, you're going to stay here and guard him. Mina and I are going to head home to my father and fill him in. I'll ask Tate to come help you keep watch tonight. The two of you can switch off, and in the morning, I'll send new replacements."

Dorian stepped to the front of the stainless-steel counter I was leaning against. He hoisted himself up on it and gave Peter a look of death. "Sounds good to me. And don't worry, this guy isn't going anywhere."

"Good. Break his bones if he tries to run but don't kill him," I said, hoping to get a good rise out of Peter before I left. It worked. His face paled, and I enjoyed that it was because of something I'd said.

"Understood," Dorian insisted with a nod of his head as he folded his arms over his solid chest.

"Tate will be here within the hour," Eli said as he placed a hand on my hip and steered me toward the open basement window.

"I'll be here waiting for him," Dorian insisted.

When Eli and I made it through the window, he bent at the waist to scoop up the files I'd left there. Neither one of us spoke until we were halfway down the driveway, each of us lost in the haze of our own thoughts.

"I can't believe you're really going through with this," he said as he shook his head.

Of course, that would be the first thing he said. "What choice do we have?" I asked, glancing at him as we continued through the woods that lined Peter's driveway.

"There has to be something else. I just need time to think about it. This can't be the only option."

I didn't say so, but I knew it was. There was no way in hell I'd let anyone else take my place. This was my decision, and Eli was going to have to deal with it if he wanted to save our pack.

15

Once we made it back to Mirror Lake Trailer Park, Eli pulled into his driveway and cut the engine. The ride home had been a long and silent one.

"I guess I should go wake my dad and tell him what's going on," Eli said with a sigh. I imagined the conversation would be both good and bad, considering we'd found Glenn and then let him be taken by vampires.

I glanced in the side mirror of Eli's truck, looking at Gran's trailer. It didn't look like there were any lights on. I was fine with that. I didn't feel like being questioned by anyone about where I had been or why I looked so upset.

"It would be best if you didn't come with me. He's not going to be happy when he finds out I let Glenn slip away again," Eli said. He gripped the steering wheel until his knuckles turned white. "You're more than welcome to go inside my place and wait on me if you don't feel like heading home. As a matter of fact, I'd prefer it. I'm not ready for you to go home yet." Raw emotion hung in his voice.

I glanced at him. Something about him seemed torn and beautiful. While I'd be lying if I said Eli hadn't always been handsome, I couldn't deny that this was the handsomest I have ever seen him. I knew it was because I could see how much he truly cared about me reflected in his green eyes right then.

I licked my lips. "I'm not ready to go home yet either."

Eli pulled the keys out of the ignition. "I'll be there in a little bit."

"Are you sure you don't want me to come with you?" I asked as I popped the passenger door open and climbed out.

"No, I'll be all right. It won't take me long. Take these inside," Eli said as he gathered the files he'd tossed on the seat between us. "And find the moonshine. I could use a drink." He winked.

I rolled my eyes as I took the files. "Fine, but it doesn't mean I'm drinking with you."

"Just one sip. We have to celebrate everything we learned tonight, don't we?"

I wasn't sure if what we'd learned was worthy of celebrating.

Eli headed for his parents' place, and I started up the wooden steps to his front door. I let myself inside and flipped on a couple of lights before moving to the kitchen. I set the files on the counter and reached into the cabinet above the stove for a jar of moonshine, then grabbed two plastic cups. As I set them on the counter, my eyes drifted to the files. The urge to flip through them was overwhelming, but I ignored it, opting to wait until Eli came back. I wasn't sure I wanted to see whatever was inside while alone. A large part of me was positive the contents held the power to destroy me.

I filled one of the plastic cups with water and downed half of it in a few gulps. My entire body trembled as the night caught up with me. I couldn't believe Glenn had been at Peter's the entire time. I couldn't believe we hadn't been able to rescue him. Instead we'd watched him be taken by vampires. Ones who were going to harvest his blood so they could mix it with ginseng and create a potent drug.

Glenn didn't deserve that. No one did.

My eyes zeroed in on the spines of the files, counting how many there were. Six. That meant there were six members of the pack had gone missing right under our noses.

Sickness twisted through my stomach.

I finished the rest of my water and then unscrewed the cap to Eli's moonshine. I poured myself a little. My hand shook as I brought it to my lips. Squeezing my eyes closed, I took a big gulp. It burned like a mother, but I found I didn't mind. Not really. With my cup in hand, I walked to the couch and switched on the TV. I remember him saying he didn't have cable or satellite, but he had Netflix. That was enough for me. I flipped through it until I found a cheesy comedy I hadn't seen in forever.

Laughter always was the best medicine.

When I was halfway into the movie, Eli came through the front door. I tried to gauge his mood from the expression on his face to determine if the conversation between him and his dad had gone well, but he wasn't giving me much to go off.

"Moonshine is on the counter," I said and then held up my cup. "I've already had a little."

"You haven't looked at the files yet? I figured that would

be the first thing you did," he said as he started toward the kitchen counter where I'd left them.

"I didn't want to look at them alone," I admitted. "How did things go with your dad?"

"Good and bad. Exactly like I figured they would," Eli said as he poured himself a cup. "I think he's just a hard man to please when it comes to this situation."

"Why do you say that?"

Eli swiped the files off the counter and walked to the couch. I straightened myself up and tucked my feet beneath me, giving him room. "He's upset we let Glenn slip through our fingers again, but especially that we allowed him to be taken by vampires. He's also pretty upset we decided to strike a deal with Peter. He doesn't want you to give yourself over to him any more than I do, but he also doesn't see a better solution. Looks like I'm in the minority when it comes to that. He believes, same as you do, we need someone on the inside. He also thinks you're perfect for the job." Eli lifted his cup as though he was toasting to me, but the frown on his face said otherwise.

I squashed the excitement I felt from hearing his father had so much confidence in me and focused on Eli. "And what do you think?"

"I think he's right. I just wish I didn't have to send you in alone. I can't even think about it, Mina. It makes me sick to my stomach." Worry creased the area between his brows as his green eyes darkened.

I understood how he felt. If the shoe was on the other foot, there would be no way I'd want Eli to go in without me. I placed a hand on his arm and squeezed. He reached for it and interlaced his fingers with mine. I closed my eyes as the feeling of his warmth seeped through me. His touch felt good. Calming, soothing. Exactly what I needed.

"I know there isn't any other way," Eli insisted. "Talking with my dad made me realize that. We just have to figure out what you need to do once you're inside."

"We should probably talk to Dorian about that," I said. "He seems good at making plans."

"It's definitely his forte."

I nodded toward the files in his lap. "While he's preoccupied with something else, maybe we should take a look at the files and see what we can learn. There might be something in them that could help us decide on a plan of action."

"You're probably right," Eli said. He split the stack in two. "You look through this half and I'll look through the other."

"Sounds good to me."

Eli passed me three folders. They were thicker than I thought they should be. How many tests had Peter ran on each wolf?

Knots the size of my fist twisted my stomach. I pulled in a deep breath as I prepared myself to open the first file. I had no idea who was going to be inside or what I'd find when I read through its pages. As I flipped open the top file of my stack my heart stalled out. There was a picture of Old Man Winter. He was strapped to the chair I saw in the center of Peter's basement. A breakdown had been typed beside his picture, stating he was subject number three. It listed his height, weight, and age. There was also a breakdown of his blood type and whether he had passed a multitude of stress tests.

I drifted back to his picture as shock continued to ripple

through me. I couldn't believe the old man hadn't gone out to the woods to die or ran away like everyone thought. Instead he'd been abducted by the same people who'd taken Glenn and Violet.

How could we have been so blind?

I flipped through the other pages in the file, checking to see what other information Peter had gathered on Old Man Winter. There wasn't much I could make out. The majority of it was scientific mumbo-jumbo and charts I couldn't read.

"I can't believe this," I said, flipping the file around so Eli could see Winter's picture. "Look who else Peter had in his basement."

Eli glanced up from the folder he was staring at. Something beyond disbelief flickered through his eyes. It took me a second to name the emotion I was seeing.

Sorrow.

Icy tendrils of panic brushed across my skin. "What?"

"I can't believe it either," he said as he flipped his folder around to show me the file he was reading. My eyes focused on the picture without ever reading the name.

It was of my mother.

My stomach clenched as I inhaled a small breath while staring at her picture. This meant she hadn't left us; she'd been taken. My eyes shifted to the stats listed beside her picture and zeroed in on the first line.

Subject number one.

My heart thundered inside my chest as I struggled to breathe. This changed everything.

All the cruel words and nasty thoughts that had plagued my mind since the day she'd left pelted me. I thought of my dad and how broken he'd been for years thinking she'd walked away because of his disability, because of his drinking. I thought of Gracie and how she'd been practically raised by Gran and me, motherless, thinking her mom didn't want her.

Then I thought of my mom being taken by vampires to have her blood harvested so they could get high.

Livid didn't even touch how I felt.

In that moment I was glad I'd volunteered to be taken in by Regina's goons, because now I had more motivation and desire to see her place burned to the damn ground.

Not only was I going to rescue Glenn, but I was going to rescue every other pack member held captive by Regina, including my mother. And if I were to find out my mom hadn't lived through the harvesting, I was going to kill the bitch that had taken her from me.

And I was going to enjoy it.

16

I woke the next morning to the sound of my cell ringing. A dull ache pulsed through my head as bright light from the window streamed in and the ringing continued. I wasn't sure how much I had to drink last night but knew at some point I'd walked home. I remembered Eli asking me to stay. I remembered telling him I just wanted to be alone. He'd understood, especially after what we'd found in the files.

Not only was there a file for my mother and Old Man Winter, but there were files for a few others from the pack too. One of them being Felicia's babies' daddy. The other three were guys who'd been with the pack a short while before they disappeared. We'd thought they weren't the type to settle in Mirror Lake and be a part of a pack; we thought they were drifters.

How wrong we'd been.

I opened one eye and reached for my cell. Ridley's name

lit my screen. The sight of it was like cold water being splashed over me. Instantly I was awake.

"Hey," I answered. Sleep clung to my words, weighing them down.

I forced myself into a sitting position, knowing Ridley would only call if she had information for me that might help get Violet's wolf back.

"Morning sunshine." Ridley chuckled. "You sound rough. Late night?"

"You have no idea." I adjusted my pillow behind my head and leaned against it. "Did you find something? Please tell me you learned of a way to reverse what's happened to Violet."

"I did. Well, my aunt and I did. We found a spell. The problem is we can't perform it until the full moon. Thankfully, that's in two nights."

Two nights? I couldn't believe the full moon was upon me already. Time flew when I was stressed the hell out, I guess.

"That's great. Is there anything that needs to be gathered for it? Anything the pack needs to do in preparation?" I asked.

"I think my aunt and I have everything. All we need is the full moon."

"What does the spell call for?" I was curious as to what they planned to do to Violet. She'd been through enough already; hopefully this wouldn't hurt her.

"We need to invoke the power of the moon goddess into a spelled liquid meant to find things that once were lost. There's no guarantee it will work, but we can at least try."

We had to try. I couldn't sit around and let Violet continue to suffer. This needed to be fixed.

"What about the cost? Has that been determined?" I knew it was the first thing I'd be asked when I told anyone of the spell Ridley had found. Also, curiosity was pulling at my insides.

"My aunt said that's something between her and your alpha."

"Oh. Okay." I didn't like the sound of that, but there wasn't much I could say about it.

"We'll meet you and your pack at your usual ceremony grounds the night of the full moon to perform the spell," Ridley said. "You get some rest. It sounds like you need it." There was a slight chuckle to her tone. Could she tell I had a hangover?

"Thanks," I said.

"No problem. Call me sometime. I'd love to hang out."

"I will. See you soon," I said before I hung up.

I set my phone on my nightstand and thought about the spell Ridley found. I hoped it worked.

Clanking in the kitchen captured my attention. Gran was up and cooking.

I picked my phone back up and checked the time. It was after ten in the morning. I couldn't remember when I'd last slept this late. My gaze drifted to Gracie's bed. It was empty. There was no sign of Winston either. As much as he annoyed me sometimes, I sure could use a little loving from the fluffy thing.

I forced myself out of bed and down the hall. Gran was in the kitchen at the stove like I'd expected.

"Morning. You got in late last night," Gran said without looking at me. Her words were clipped and harsh.

Had I been loud about coming in? The chances were pretty high, considering how much moonshine I'd had to drink.

"I did," I said as I rubbed my temples in an effort to ward off the dull ache building behind my eyes from the brightness of the florescent light in the kitchen. "It was a really long night."

"I'm sure." Gran shifted to face me. Her lips were pressed into a thin line as her eyes gave me a once-over. "I can still smell the remnants of it on you."

Her tone had my heart skipping a beat. She was pissed I'd come home drunk. Guilt sloshed through me as I suddenly felt no better than my dad.

I looked to the living room, trying to avoid Gran's pissed off gaze and spotted Dad passed out on the couch with an empty bottle of rum near him. Gracie was in the recliner.

Shit.

"I'm sorry. It won't happen again," I promised without looking at Gran.

"It better not. It's bad enough I have one drunk coming in at all hours of the night; I don't need my granddaughter coming home drunk too," she whispered as she shook her spatula at me. While her voice was low, I was sure Gracie could hear every word she said from where she sat with Winston perched in her lap.

Embarrassment didn't even come close to naming what I felt.

"I know," I said as I dipped my gaze to the linoleum floor beneath my feet. "It won't happen again."

"Good. Now, tell me what has you drinking so heavily. What's going on, Mina?" Gran insisted as she turned back to the stove and continued cooking.

I stepped to the counter and leaned against it, checking out what she was cooking.

Hamburger meat.

Cans of tomatoes and beans stood on the counter next to the crockpot. It must be chili night. Normally, I loved Gran's chili. Not this morning, though. The thought of it had my stomach souring and my mouth filling with saliva.

"I can't tell you everything," I said as I grabbed a glass down from the cabinet near the sink. I filled it with tap water and chugged, hoping it would get rid of my headache. "But, I can tell you I spoke with Ridley this morning. The Caraway witches are going to help us with Violet."

"What is it they plan to do?" Gran asked as she pulled out a cutting board and diced an onion.

"She said they plan to invoke the power of the moon goddess into a spelled liquid meant to find what's been lost. They have to do it on the night of the full moon, which I can't believe is two nights away. She also said they'd meet us at the ceremony grounds then."

Gran scraped the diced-up onion into the crockpot and reached for a clove of garlic. I studied her face, gauging to see whether she thought what the Caraway witches planned would work. She didn't give any indication.

"Do you think it will work?" I asked when I grew tired of the silence.

"It might. I can't say it won't, but I can't say it will either. It seems plausible, though. Especially since they would basically be putting a piece of what was lost inside a potion.

When Violet drinks it, it should be enough to help her wolf find its way back to her."

I set my empty glass in the sink. "Makes sense."

"I know that's not all that's going on with you," Gran said as her eyes sought out mine. "Is there anything you can tell me about what it is you've been doing with Eli?"

"I wish I could, but I can't. It's all pack-related stuff. I can tell you something about me and Eli though," I said. Nervous butterflies burst through the pit of my stomach as I thought about how to word what I was going to say next. "I broke things off with Alec. Eli and I...well..."

Gran's eyes widened as her hand flew to her mouth. "You two imprinted, didn't you?"

My teeth sank into my bottom lip. All I could do was nod.

"Oh, Mina! I knew it! I'm so happy for you! I knew it would happen between you. I've never seen a bond so strong between two members of the pack before. The two of you were destined to be together. It was written in the stars, sweet girl."

While I wasn't sure I believed we'd been written in the stars, I couldn't deny there had been a certain type of chemistry building between us for years.

"I knew working on whatever it is you are together would bring you close enough to finally realize it," Gran insisted. "It's a blessing in disguise."

I swallowed hard. That was where she was wrong; there was no blessing in disguise anywhere in this situation. She would understand if she knew what I'd learned last night.

I folded my arms over my chest and stared at her. "There's something else I need to tell you. Actually, it might be better if I showed you." I headed back to my bedroom, remembering I'd brought the file on my mother home with me last night. I'd shoved it underneath my mattress to look at later in-depth.

Once I grabbed it, I headed back to the kitchen to show it to Gran. She deserved to know.

"While I can't tell you a whole lot about what Eli and I have been working on, I don't think it would be fair of me not to show this to you." I held the file out to her as my eyes shifted to Gracie in the recliner. She was watching TV while stroking Winston's soft fur, oblivious to Gran and me. "But it's not something Gracie should know about. Not yet anyway." Maybe not ever if I didn't find our mother alive.

Gran took the folder from me. Worry etched itself into the features of her face as her eyes grew dull. "What is this?"

"Open it. Look at the first page." My heart hammered inside my chest as I waited for her to do as I said.

Gran's hand shook as she opened the folder. I knew she realized what she was holding. Seconds later she slumped against the kitchen counter as though the sight of my mother had been a physical blow to her. "Oh my."

"She never ran away," I whispered. "She was abducted. By the same people who took Violet."

Tears glistened in Gran's eyes. "All this time," she whispered.

The sight of her tears brought on tears of my own. I knew how she felt. Unbelieving. Stupid for not having known. Sorry beyond words for thinking ill of her for so many years.

"I know," I whispered as I took the folder from her and wrapped my arms around her.

"Do you know where she's being kept?" Gran whispered.

"Not exactly, but I'm going to find out," I promised.

"Be careful, Mina. Please promise me you'll be careful."

"Always."

I meant what I said, but I also wasn't a fortune teller. I could promise I'd be careful until I was blue in the face, but I couldn't predict whether I'd come out of what I already agreed to safe and well.

Gran squeezed me tighter. I closed my eyes and relaxed into the warmth and love she sent my way through her bear hug.

17

The next two days passed the way time always does when you're waiting on something important to happen—slowly. I drank plenty of water and ate the food Gran shoved my way. I tried not to think about how the spell might not work or how it would mean Violet's wolf might be gone for good, but it was hard not to.

My stomach somersaulted as I made my way through the woods, following behind those of my pack. The Caraway witches were supposed to meet us at the ceremony grounds, but also tonight Eli and I imprinting needed to be acknowledged. Even though everyone in the pack knew about it, it still needed to be made official.

We had to be bonded by blood, bite, and soul.

Eli squeezed my hand in his when we reached the clearing of the ceremony grounds. Ridley and her aunt, Rowena, were already present. Ridley smiled and gave me a slight wave.

"I didn't think we would have an audience beyond the

pack for our imprinting ceremony," Eli insisted, his eyes having landed on Ridley and her aunt as well.

"Me neither," I said as we reached the fire pit. "From the look on your dad's face, I don't think he thought we would either. Maybe they're early?"

"I wonder what he plans to do," Eli whispered. "Think he'll let them watch or make them leave?"

"I don't know," I said as I continued to stare at our alpha, watching to see what he did next.

"Thank you, both of you, for coming tonight and for everything you've done in an attempt to help one of our own. Tonight is a special night. Not only because we hope to heal one of our young ones and bring back her wolf, but also because we have something beautiful to celebrate," Eli's dad said to all of us. "We'll let the witches do what they must and then celebrate what needs to be celebrated before we run."

Each member of the pack nodded and murmured their agreement. Our alpha nodded to the witches, asking them to continue. I watched as Violet was helped to the area she'd sat in last month, sipping her tea while hoping to become moon kissed. Her cuts were nearly healed and her bruises almost faded, but her ankle was still mangled enough for her to have difficulty walking. I sent up a silent prayer to the moon goddess, asking that whatever the witches did tonight brought Violet's wolf back to her so she could be healed.

Ridley's aunt stepped to where Violet was. I continued to look on as Ridley set out the contents of a silver silk bag she carried. A bowl, a bell, jars of brightly colored powders, a bottle of water, and a stick of incense.

A hush fell over the pack as we watched Rowena Caraway do her thing.

Powders were sprinkled on the ground around Violet. Incense was lit. Water was poured into a ceramic bowl and placed in a spot close to Violet while still able to reflect the full moon. Words were spoken under Rowena's breath, making it difficult to hear. I'd never witnessed a witch use magic before, but I swore it should have been more exciting than it was. I'd been expecting harsh winds, lightning, or even a downpour of rain to burst from the sky, but nothing of that nature happened. In fact, things were so anticlimactic the only thing that signified Rowena's spell was complete was Ridley ringing a bell three times.

Either TV had given me a biased view of witchcraft, or this spell wasn't nearly as fancy as I'd thought.

"Now remember," Rowena said as she swiped a few strands of her dark hair away from her eyes. "I can't guarantee this spell will work. I can't even tell you how long it might take before you see results if it does. This isn't something I've done before," Rowena insisted as she passed Violet the bowl.

Maybe it hadn't been plain water inside, but rather the potion they were supposed to invoke the moon goddess into.

"Take three sips of equal size," she instructed as she waved some incense around like a wand. "By the power of three times three, so mote it be."

Again I expected a crash of thunder or something fantastical to happen but nothing did.

Violet seemed still as broken as she had. I stared at her, waiting for something to happen. A miracle.

Ridley moved to grab a bottle with a cork on the top and a tiny funnel from inside her bag. She uncorked the bottle and placed the funnel inside before handing it to her aunt.

Rowena carefully poured the remaining liquid from the bowl into the bottle.

"All she needed was three sips," Rowena said. "You should hold onto the rest of this case you need it sometime in the future."

Did she know what we were up against? Did she know members of our pack had been abducted and could possibly have been severed from their wolf like Violet?

Rowena replaced the cork on the bottle once she finished filling it to the rim and stepped to where Gran stood. "If you need to use this again, make sure you do it beneath a full moon. You might have to adjust the dose, depending on how long the person's wolf has been severed from them. I gave Violet only three sips because her wolf has not been lost long. For someone else, you may need to repeat monthly until the wolf is found."

"Thank you," Gran said as she took the bottle.

"You're welcome," Rowena said before turning her attention back to our alpha. "All I ask in return for what I've done here tonight is a favor when I need it in the future."

"Done," the alpha agreed without hesitation. "Thank you."

"You're most welcome. We will see ourselves out. Enjoy your run," Rowena said as she placed a hand on Ridley's shoulder and steered her toward the well-worn path that wove through the woods.

"Sylvie, go ahead and take the young ones home," Eli's dad said. Sylvie nodded and rounded up the children.

My eyes fell back to Violet. She sat with her back straight and her legs crossed in front of her. There was a dazed look about her. Was she worried the spell might not work? Or was it already working, and she was lost in her mind like when her wolf was first found and she'd been moon kissed?

"We'll let the witches' magic work its wonders on Violet while we continue on with the night's events," Eli's dad insisted. He motioned for Eli and me to step forward. We did, me slightly more hesitant than Eli. "Tonight, we celebrate the imprinting of my son, Eli Vargas, and Mina Ryan."

The pack burst into whistles, howls, and shouts of congratulations. A wide smile spread across my face at the sound of them, my nerves suddenly forgotten.

"As is tradition, now that these two have imprinted with one another and their souls are bonded, they must be bonded in two more ways—of blood and bite—to make it official," the alpha continued. "Eli, Mina, please extend your right hand."

I did as I was told, knowing what was coming next. The alpha took Eli's hand first. He reached for a knife in his pocket and held the silver blade high in the air. "Thank you, moon goddess, for bringing these two together. I now will join them by blood in your honor."

I watched as he slashed a small cut across the palm of Eli's hand before moving to do the same to me. The pain from the small incision was a lot less than I thought it would be. In fact, I barely flinched.

"Palm to palm, please," the alpha instructed. Eli and I pressed our palms together. Cut to cut. Blood to blood. "May the moon goddess bless this union for all eternity," Eli's dad said as he cupped his hands around our touching palms.

My eyes locked with Eli's. The corners of his lips twisted upward to form an adorable smile. I wanted to kiss him but restrained myself. Instead I focused on the warmth traveling from where our palms touched. Our blood mingled until there was no distinguishing where his began and mine ended. We were united, and I loved the rush of pure bliss coursing through me because of it.

How could I have ever fought against what I felt for him?

"Now I ask that you all shed your clothing and shift for the final part of the ceremony," Eli's dad insisted as he released our hands.

I pulled my palm away from Eli's. The cut had already healed. Nothing remained besides a streak of blood across my skin. My eyes locked with Eli's. The look in his eyes had goose bumps flaring to life across my skin. He wanted me as much as I wanted him. I smiled at him, delirious at this beautiful moment, before I shed my clothes. I was ready for the next part of the ceremony, ready for us to be united as one in every way as we were meant to.

"I love you," Eli whispered as he peeled off his clothes.

"I love you too," I said without hesitation.

Once I was naked and free of all silver jewelry, I called on my wolf. She stood in the shadows of my mind, eagerly waiting to be set free. This moment was for her, too. She knew what was to come next, and she was as excited as I was to be united with her wolf.

When our pack had shifted, Eli and I were nudged close together by the alpha. I knew what I was supposed to do, I'd seen it before. Facing Eli, I touched his nose with my own. His warm breath fanned my face seconds before he nuzzled his way to the side of my neck. I closed my eyes as I curled my lips back, revealing my sharp teeth. The alpha howled, giving the signal and both of us bit down on one another. My mouth filled with the coppery taste of Eli's blood, and then I released my hold on him. It was a little nibble, not a gouging bite, but we both knew we were supposed to break skin for it to hold.

As soon as I pulled back, Eli did the same. The pack released a howl of excitement; Eli and I were now bonded by blood, bite, and soul.

Our alpha broke into a run, heading for the woods, and the rest of the pack followed him. Eli and I hung back, enjoying our moment as we nuzzled one another before we ran to catch up with the others.

Wind whipped through my fur. It stung my eyes as I pushed my legs faster while running beside Eli. Never had I felt so content, so free. I lost myself in the present moment. The feel of the ground beneath my paws and the beautiful moonlight against my fur. For once, I wasn't thinking about Glenn or Violet, my mom, or Peter locked in a cage where he belonged after all he'd done. I wasn't thinking of offing Regina or how I'd offered myself up to be taken by her goons.

I was only thinking about the run and my beautiful moment with Eli.

THANK YOU

Thank you for reading *Moon Severed*, I hope you enjoyed it! Please consider leaving an honest review at your point of purchase. Reviews help me in so many ways!

If you would like to know when my next novel is available, you can sign up for my newsletter here:
https://jennifersnyderbooks.com/want-the-latest/
Also, feel free to reach out and tell me your thoughts about the novel. I'd love to hear from you!
Email me at: jennifersnyder04@gmail.com

To see a complete up-to-date list of my novels, please take a moment to visit this page:
http://jennifersnyderbooks.com/book-list/

MINA'S STORY CONTINUES IN...

MOON BURNED

Mirror Lake Wolves - Book Four

AVAILABLE NOW!

Sometimes a sacrifice is the only option...

Time is ticking. The fate of Mina's pack rests heavily on her shoulders. The moment she must give herself over to Regina's vampire goons looms closer and it's all she can do to appear strong. Focusing on Dorian and Eli's plan and the knowledge she'll be taking Regina down soon is all that keeps her moving forward.

But when the plan is botched, and someone else is taken with Mina to the city, she isn't sure she's strong enough to save him and do all she set out to.

Death and destruction will touch the werewolves of Mirror Lake. Who will remain standing after the smoke clears?

Return to Mirror Lake in the fourth book of the Mirror Lake Wolves series and hold on tight because things are about to get intense!

Please Keep Reading for a sneak peek...

ONE

My legs moved across soft sheets as the low hum of an air conditioner made its way to my ears. I rolled over causing a familiar masculine scent clinging to the sheets to waft to my nose. My lips twisted into a wide smile.

Eli.

I could feel him beside me. His presence was strong. It pulsed through my veins when he was near. Two nights in a row. That was how many I'd spent with him.

Without opening my eyes, I rolled onto my side and trailed my fingers across the cool sheets between us to find him. The tips of my fingers traveled along the length of his ribs before I ventured over his toned abdomen. He stirred at the feel of my touch. I opened one eye and peeked at him. His eyes were still closed. Sun rays streaked through the thin slotted mini-blinds, illuminating his beautiful sun-kissed skin.

It was later in the morning than I thought.

My fingertips continued to trail along the ridges of his sculpted chest. I allowed myself to soak in every inch of him.

God, why had it taken me so long to accept what I'd always felt for him? How could I have been so stubborn? My stomach tightened as I realized I'd denied myself so much time with him. Years.

I'd been stupid.

"It's way too early to be thinking as hard as you are over there," Eli said, startling me. His voice was a low rumble that vibrated my fingertips pressed against his chest.

"So do something to distract me," I teased as I flashed him a saucy smile.

Eli arched a brow while acceptance of my challenge shifted through his eyes. "Do something to distract you, you say?"

As soon as the words left his mouth, he reached across the empty space between us and pulled me closer. His warm lips wasted no time finding their way below my earlobe to place warm kisses there. His fingertips wandered the length of my hip before making the journey to my inner thigh.

"How am I doing? Feeling distracted from your thoughts yet?" Eli asked as his teeth nibbled my earlobe.

"Mmmm, yes."

"Are you sure? Because I can always amp things up." His fingers brushed over my center in a featherlight touch.

I didn't speak. I didn't move. In fact, I could barely breathe.

Eli's warm lips trailed down my neck, across my shoulder, and along my collarbone as he moved to position himself on top of me.

"You didn't answer me. I assume that means you want me to kick it up a notch," he said.

All I could do was chuckle in response. It came out breathy and strangled sounding, but at least it was something.

"While I have you quivering beneath me, let me ask you a question." He held himself up with his forearms, his lips no longer on me. "When are you moving in so we can do this every morning?"

My stomach didn't clench like I thought it might when/if he ever asked. My heart didn't even hammer out an erratic beat. I was surprisingly calm as I stared into his bright green eyes. Until I remembered our bet. Then all I could do was grin.

"What? You look like you're up to no good," Eli said.

"How do you feel about purple? Dark purple, like maybe a plum color?"

The area between his brows scrunched together. He had no idea what I was talking about. He'd forgotten our bet.

"I ask when you can move in, and you ask how I feel about the color purple?"

"Exactly." My grin grew. "You know, it can be a sophisticated color when it has gray undertones. Perfect for bedroom walls."

He opened his mouth to respond, but the sound of my phone ringing had his lips clamping shut.

I knew who it was. Just as I knew she was probably freaking out because she'd woke up to me not home again.

Eli rolled off me as I reached for my phone. Gracie's name and number lit the screen.

I knew it would be her.

"It's Gracie," I said as I sat up. "I should answer. If I don't she'll just call repeatedly hoping to wake me up with the ringing."

"Go for it," Eli insisted. "The sooner you answer her, the sooner you can answer me." His green eyes glittered as his lips twisted into a crooked grin.

"Hello?" I said as I answered Gracie's call, ignoring Eli's adorable smirk and the way it had my stomach feeling alive with butterflies.

"Where are you? Did you spend the night with Eli again?" Gracie asked, her tone sharp.

"Good morning to you too." Heavy sarcasm dripped from my words. I rolled my eyes. It was amazing how demanding and snotty she could be first thing in the morning.

"You're supposed to be here. Winston has his vet appointment this morning."

Was it really that late already? It couldn't be. I glanced at the window, trying to judge the time by how much sunlight streamed through the blinds.

"What time is it?" I asked.

A huff filtered through the phone. "It's eight. We're supposed to be at the vet's office before eight thirty. You said you'd take me. Winston needs these shots."

"I am taking you. Calm down. I'll be there in a second."

"Hurry up," Gracie said before she hung up on me.

"Wow. She sounds like a pistol first thing in the morning." Eli chuckled.

"She is," I said as I rolled out of bed to get dressed.

"Where do you think you're going?" Eli asked. He wrapped his arms around my waist and pulled me back into bed with him. "You didn't answer my question yet."

"I have to go. You heard Gracie."

"Nope. You're not leaving until you answer me," Eli insisted as he climbed on top of me, pinning me in place. "When are you moving in so I can wake up beside you every morning?" He buried his face into the crook of my neck and skimmed his tongue along the skin there. It tickled.

A laugh bellowed from deep in my chest. "Is that all you care about? Waking up beside me so you can get some action?"

"You know that's not true."

I did, but it felt good to hear him say it.

"I want action at night too." He grinned.

"Funny."

I maneuvered myself out from under him and slipped out of bed. He moved around on the mattress behind me, but I ignored him as I reached for my clothes on the floor.

"Don't make me beg," he surprised me by saying.

"I don't have any intentions to," I said as I pulled on my panties.

Eli shifted around until his arms were positioned behind his head, causing his biceps to flex and his abs to tighten. I really liked when they did that.

"Really? Because it seems like you do." A ghost of a smile hung loose on his lips. "You know, I wouldn't expect anything less from you. I know you well enough to know you're going to drag this out for as long as you see fit."

"Then why are we having this conversation?" I asked as I fastened my bra. My teeth sank into my bottom lip to suppress a smile.

He definitely had me pegged.

"Because of that right there." Eli grinned as he pointed at

me. "The sheer amount of satisfaction you get from it is sexy as hell."

My face heated. He truly did have me figured out.

"Whatever," I said as I rolled my eyes and reached for my tank top. I slipped it over my head and then grabbed my cut-off shorts. "I really do have to go. Winston's appointment is in a few minutes. Gracie is going to have my head if I make her late."

"I guess you better get going then." He stretched out on his bed, tightening the muscles of his abdomen as a sexy look festered in his green eyes.

"I know what you're trying to do," I said.

"I'm not trying to do anything."

"You are. You're trying to make yourself look so irresistible I won't leave."

A shit-eating grin spread across his face. "Is it working?"

"Wouldn't you like to know." I reached for my cell and crammed it into my back pocket.

"It's working. Oh yeah. I know it is," he said.

"Confident much?"

"In this instance you're damn right." He flexed his arm muscles, making lust uncurl within my stomach. If I didn't get out of here, I was going to jump him and then Gracie would be pissed because she most definitely would be late.

"Jesus," I said as I bent at the waist, pulling my eyes away from him and searching for my sandals. Somehow I was only able to find one.

"How long is this appointment supposed to take?" Eli asked. "I'm off today, and I really want to spend as much time with you as possible." All sense of teasing and playfulness had evaporated from his tone.

I knew why. Tonight I was supposed to hand myself over to Regina's goons.

"An hour tops?" I said as I got down on my knees to look beneath his bed for my missing sandal. It was there. How it got under there was another story though. "It shouldn't take me too long."

"Good," he said.

I extended my arm as far as I could underneath his bed. I was still barely able to reach my sandal. "Why? Do you have something planned?" I asked as I swiped hair away from my eyes.

"It's possible."

"Well, I hope it isn't anything with a time limit. I'm not exactly sure how long this is going to take. I mean Shane's brother, Peter, is the vet and it's safe to say he's not going in to work today."

Or any day in the foreseeable future for that matter, considering we hadn't figured out what to do with him after tonight yet. He was still in the basement of his house locked inside a cage he'd once used to house numerous werewolves from our pack against their will.

Karma was a bitch sometimes, but I happened to like her.

"Winston will get seen today. Don't worry. Peter isn't the only vet at the clinic," Eli said.

"Since when?" I asked as I slipped on my sandals.

"Since about a week ago."

"How do you know? Keeping tabs on the place?"

Eli sat up in bed. "Sort of. The new vet happens to be a member of the Montevallo family."

I arched a brow as I stared at him. "When did they get back into town?"

I'd never met a member of the Montevallo family before, but it didn't mean I knew nothing about them. They were the only vampire family allowed to live in Mirror Lake. I wasn't sure why but knew it had something to do with the Caraway witches. The only other thing I knew about the family of vampires was they owned a gigantic mansion in town and every couple of decades found their way back to it.

"Around the same time one of them started working at the vet clinic," Eli said, pulling me from my thoughts.

"Why didn't you mention anything sooner?"

"I didn't realize you'd be interested."

I could see his point.

"What about Peter? What does everyone think happened to him? He's been gone for over a week." It hadn't occurred to me until now how suspicious that might seem. Especially after the death of his brother, Drew.

The thought of Drew had my skin prickling with anxiety. I still couldn't get the image of Eli snapping his neck out of my head. It would forever haunt me.

"Dorian had him call in sick," Eli insisted.

"You can't be serious."

"I am. Why?"

"Because that's not a good excuse. It's summer. Who gets sick in summer?" I asked thinking Dorian should have had him say he needed to take some time off. It would have been more believable.

Eli slipped out of bed and reached for a pair of boxers he'd tossed on the floor last night. "Lots of people."

"It doesn't seem believable to me."

"Only because you know the truth. No one else does. To them Peter being sick is the truth." Eli stepped to where I was and wrapped his arms around my waist, pulling me into him. "Now, go take that cute little puppy to the vet for his shots and then get your sexy ass back here. Like I said, I've got plans for us today."

Something soft and sweet reflected in his eyes. Whatever he had planned would be memorable. It was written all over his face.

"Okay," I said as I stood on the tips of my toes to peck his lips. Eli held tight when I pulled away. "I have to go."

"Then you better kiss me goodbye the right way. Not some little cheap peck on the lips."

The quiver in his voice nearly broke me. He was worried his time with me was running short. Didn't he know this wasn't the last time he would see me? I wouldn't allow it to be. Regina had stolen too much from me, from my family, from my pack. There was no way in hell I'd let her take my life too. It wasn't happening.

Interlocking my hands behind Eli's head, I stood on tiptoes and crushed my lips to his. He allowed me to think I was in control for a few sporadic heartbeats before he decided to take over. Lust coiled through my stomach as he skimmed his tongue across my lips, willing them to part wider. My body trembled in reaction. His fingertips dug into the flesh of my hips, pressing me against him until I could feel exactly how much he was enjoying our kiss.

By the time I managed to pull away, I was breathless.

"There. Now that was a goodbye kiss," Eli insisted as he released his hold on me.

"Yeah. It was. I'll see you in a little while," I said as I dizzily walked out of his room.

When I exited Eli's trailer and stepped into the bright

morning sunlight, the air was already too warm. Humidity weighed it down, making it hard to breathe. When I was halfway to Gran's trailer, a good layer of sweat already glistened across my skin.

My cell chimed with a new text. I let out a breath of air, knowing it was most likely Gracie wondering where the hell I was. I thought to ignore it but then decided against it. A name I hadn't been expecting to see lit my screen.

Alec.

My heart beat erratically inside my chest at the sight of his name. I hadn't spoken to him since breaking up with him, which he had handled too well.

Hey. I don't know if you're awake yet, but I wanted to let you know I was thinking about you. I know we're not dating or whatever anymore, but I meant what I said when I said I still want you in my life. Think we can still be friends?

How was I supposed to answer? Alec knew my secret. He knew my pack's secret. As much as I wanted to be friends with him, I wasn't sure it was possible. He knew too much.

I crammed my phone into my back pocket again and continued home, knowing I'd eventually reply but also knowing it wouldn't be anytime soon. Right now Gracie was waiting, and I was curious to see the new vet at the Mirror Lake Veterinary Clinic.

TWO

I expected Gracie to be on the front steps with Winston sitting in her lap when I walked up, but she wasn't. She wasn't in the living room either.

Apparently she wasn't in as big of a rush as she'd let on.

Dad was in the living room, though. I could tell from the empty bottles scattered around him he'd been on the couch all night, drinking himself into oblivion. The week after the full moon was always hardest on him. His pain was back in full force, and he was looking for ways to drown it out again.

Gran stood at the kitchen sink, hand washing the dishes from breakfast.

"Good morning," she said as she glanced over her shoulder at me. "I wasn't sure you would make it in time to take Gracie to the vet's office."

"Here I am. Where is she?"

"In her room."

I opened my mouth to yell for her, but Dad rolled over in

his sleep and mumbled something about Mom. It had my train of thought ceasing immediately.

"Today's going to be a rough one. He's been talking nonstop about her in his sleep," Gran said with a frown as she glanced at him from where she stood.

"Probably because she disappeared around this time of year," I said *probably*, but I knew without a doubt today was the day she'd been taken so many years ago.

It seemed fitting this would be the day I began my search for her by sacrificing myself to the same vampires who'd taken her.

"You're probably right. The days have blurred together so much, the years too. It's sad, but I can hardly pinpoint when she left."

I could. I knew the exact date, but I didn't say so.

"We might never have to hear him mumble about missing her again after tonight." I regretted the words as soon as I said them.

The plate Gran was washing slipped from her hands. It clanked in the sink. "Why? What are you planning?"

"I'm leaving to find her tonight."

I knew I wasn't supposed to tell anyone because it pertained to pack business, but how could I not tell Gran something? I didn't want her to worry when she couldn't find me. I didn't want her to think she'd done something wrong or that I'd ran away. I didn't want to hurt her. I also didn't want to hurt Gracie. Which meant, in case this thing went longer than a single night, I would need Gran to cover for me.

"How are you planning to do that?" Gran asked as she reached for a rag and dried off her hands. Her eyes were glued on me.

I shifted around on my feet, knowing she wasn't going to like the next words that came out of my mouth.

"I can't tell you details, but I can say there's a good chance you might not see me over the next few days. I'm headed to the city. That's where she's at. It's where everyone is," I said.

I loved Gran and the last thing I wanted to do was hurt her, but I knew my words had. She was upset I hadn't told her sooner. Her eyes told me she was worried I wouldn't come back, that she was scared something horrible might happen to me.

Still it didn't change my mind. I had to do this. No one else could. It was up to me.

"I won't ask you any more questions about it, then. I understand how pack law works." Her blue eyes locked with mine as she stepped forward and erased the space between us. She smelled like lemon dish soap as she wrapped her arms around me. "Promise me one thing. Promise me you'll be careful, okay? That you'll come back safe and sound."

We both knew her last request wasn't a promise I could make, but I did anyway. "I promise."

"Oh my God! What is with all the lovey-dovey stuff? We're going to be late!" Gracie shouted as she made her way into the kitchen with Winston in tow. His fur was wet, making him look more like a rat than a puppy.

"What did you do to him?" I asked as I untangled myself from Gran's arms.

"I gave him a bath while I was waiting on you, duh."

"Why?" I asked.

"I didn't want him to stink at his vet appointment. I want them to think I'm taking good care of him."

"Oh." It was sweet she wanted to seem like a good pet owner. Maybe this puppy would be worth keeping. Maybe he'd teach her responsibility. It seemed as though he already had.

"Are you ready? It's almost eight thirty." Gracie walked to where Gran was standing and kissed her on the cheek before putting Winston down. She grabbed his leash off the kitchen counter and bent at the waist to hook him up. "I'm supposed to get there a few minutes early to fill out paperwork since it's his first visit."

"Yeah, I'm ready. Let's go." I swiped my keys off the counter and started toward the door, following behind her.

"Do whatever it is you have planned after the appointment, Mina, but I want you and Eli at the table by six o'clock tonight ready for a family dinner. No exceptions," Gran insisted.

"Why Eli too?" I asked as I paused at the front door.

"He's family now," Gran said.

Warmth flowed through me. I loved her. I flashed her a small smile and then continued out the door after Gracie.

She was in the passenger seat when I started down the front steps. Winston sat in her lap with his tongue hanging out as he panted. Was he hot, or was he excited to be going for a ride? I couldn't tell.

"You should probably run inside and grab an old towel," I said to Gracie as I rounded the front of my car.

"Already one step ahead of you." She grinned. "I put one in here before you showed up."

"Oh, okay. Good. Do you know if he gets carsick?" I asked as I slipped behind the steering wheel.

"Not sure. Figured it would be better to be safe than sorry though," Gracie said she buckled her seat belt.

I cranked the engine of my car, waiting for it to sputter to life. For the first time in a long time, it started without hassle. Whatever Eli had done when he put the new battery in had worked wonders.

"Do you remember how to get to the clinic?" Gracie asked as she pulled up the address on her cell.

"Yeah." I scoffed, unbelieving she'd even asked. Mirror Lake was the size of my hand. Everyone knew how to get everywhere because the place was so small.

"Okay. Let's go, then," Gracie said as she made a shooing gesture with her hand.

I shifted into reverse and backed out of our driveway, frowning. She was being a bossy little thing this morning.

As I drove past Eli's trailer, I noticed him coming out the front door. He was dressed in a plain gray T-shirt, dark-washed jeans, and a pair of biker boots. His hair was still ruffled, and his eyes a little sleepy as he twirled the keys to his old beat up truck on his finger. He flashed me a panty-dropping smile and waved to Gracie as we crept by.

Where was he going? He hadn't mentioned leaving. I wondered if it had anything to do with what he had planned for us today. I hoped it wasn't anything that would overlap with Gran's dinner plans. I made a mental note to send him a text as soon as I reached the vet office, letting him know we were supposed to be at my place for dinner at six. No exceptions, as Gran had put it.

My palms began to sweat as I thought of what it would be like to have Eli over for dinner now that we were imprinted. Heat crept up my neck at the thought. God, what would my dad say during our dinner? What would Gracie say? There was no doubt in my mind the two of them would find some way to embarrass the hell out of me. I wasn't so much worried about Gran as I was Dad and Gracie. Maybe I should be, though. She could be as cantankerous as the rest of them when she wanted to be.

AVAILABLE NOW!

ABOUT THE AUTHOR

Jennifer Snyder lives in North Carolina where she spends most of her time writing New Adult and Young Adult Fiction, reading, and struggling to stay on top of housework. She is a tea lover with an obsession for Post-it notes and smooth writing pens. Jennifer lives with her husband and two children, who endure listening to songs that spur inspiration on repeat and tolerate her love for all paranormal, teenage-targeted TV shows.

To get an email whenever Jennifer releases a new title, sign up for her newsletter at https://jennifersnyderbooks.com/want-the-latest/. It's full of fun and freebies sent right to your inbox!

Find Jennifer Online!
jennifersnyderbooks.com/
jennifersnyder04@gmail.com

31372557R00120

Made in the USA
Middletown, DE
31 December 2018